THE AWAKENING OF AMELIA

MADISON GRANGER

The Awakening of Amelia

By Madison Granger

Cover design: Ravenborn Book Cover Designs, 2020

ISBN: 9798591563066
AISN: B08TLPZD25

DEDICATION

To Emily

And to all the 4S and 4N nurses,
the strongest and most courageous women
I've had the honor and pleasure
to call my friends.

ACKNOWLEDGMENTS

This book had a long journey getting to this point. What started as a stand-alone destined for a Fall release turned into a delay to be added into an anthology instead.

No regrets on my part. The anthology, *Sinners & Saints*, opened up a whole new world for me. The best part was making friends who will always be a part of my writing life.

Now, *The Awakening of Amelia* is ready to shine on her own. I've added a few scenes. expanded on others, giving the reader a little more to the story.

A huge thank you to Personal Touch Editing for making sure I stayed on track and got everything right.

Endless gratitude to Ravenborn Book Cover Designs. I can always depend on Anika to know exactly what I want.

To my Beta readers, for giving me suggestions and helpful advice to make my story the best possible.

PROLOGUE

Heart pounding and gasping for air, Amelia ran for her life—straight toward the woods. The wind whipped her long, thick hair into her face, blinding her as she fought desperately to get away from the manor house. Rocks tore at her bare feet as she struggled to keep her balance on the uneven ground. Her thin gown and wrapper were useless against the chill in the air.

Thunder reverberated in the sky as lightning strikes filled the air with an eerie light. As the storm gained momentum, so did the waves crashing against the cliffs. Huge drops of cold rain pelted Amelia as she slipped and stumbled toward the safety of the trees.

She'd been told not to venture into the forest. There were bears, wolves, and other creatures. At this point, she'd gladly seek sanctuary with wild animals before she'd go back to that house—and the threat waiting inside.

Amelia peered over her shoulder, fearful she was being followed. Someone called her name, but it could have been the wind, howling and whipping through the trees. She screamed when a limb caught her hair, a burning sting across her cheek when she yanked the small branch out, losing long strands of hair by the roots. In the struggle to free herself, Amelia wasn't paying attention to the path. The rain had quickly turned the dirt into mud, and she lost her footing. Falling hard, she fought not to scream again as she scrambled to her feet. Gulping air into her burning lungs, thankful she wasn't injured, she dashed up the path.

For the first time in longer than she could remember, Amelia prayed. All she wanted was to get out of this nightmare. She needed to get to the cliffs. If she could get there, she'd be safe.

CHAPTER 1

Three months earlier ...

Amelia punched the elevator button. As usual, the closed metal doors sat there, staring back at her, unmoving. The overhead speaker splintered the silence of the hospital halls.

"Code Blue, Nine West, Code Blue, Nine West."

The alarm made the hair on her arms rise, her heart racing. This was *so* not the way she wanted to start her six-day rotation. Jabbing the button on the wall again as if she could will the damn thing to work, she uttered a low oath.

"Crap, come on!"

It's not like they needed her up there. The night shift was probably already in the patient's room and the Code team on their way. It was instinct at this point. If there was a Code, Amelia responded. She was a nurse and a damn good one.

The elevator doors slid open, eliciting a sigh of relief from her. Raising an arched brow at the panel of numbers on the inside, she should've saved her air. She still needed to get to the ninth floor. Punching nine, she waited. Luckily, she was in the faster of the three, if any of them could be classified as fast. No matter, she was moving. It counted.

Sprinting past the Nine East nurse's station, the Unit Secretary called out, "Sixty-four!"

Well, didn't that get better?

Nine sixty-four was almost all the way down. She turned the corner, heading down the crowded hall. She really needed to start going to a gym... or carry oxygen.

Dodging extra beds, vitals machines, and linen carts, Amelia slowed down to a fast walk. People were starting to filter out of the room. Peeking in, she caught sight of Laura, the evening shift's charge nurse.

"Amelia, thank goodness. Could you help get the patient down to the Unit? We already have a room. Sixteen-oh-four."

With a nod, Amelia crossed the hallway to the rack of boxed gloves. Snapping on a pair, she helped with the last-minute details. She made sure the defibrillator was hooked up correctly and the patient's oxygen tank was in place. Grabbing the patient's chart on the way, they

4

hurried to the freight elevators in the back. Unfortunately, it was an all-too-often scene on the Telemetry floor. Heart patients were fragile, especially the non-compliant ones. They never realized how serious things were until they ended up in Critical Care. The lucky ones left the unit, only to find themselves back on the cardiac floor, right where they'd started.

It was a never-ending cycle. Most patients always returned. The nurses got to know the patients and their families way more than they wanted. She sighed inwardly. She'd become a nurse so she could help people. Lately, all she did was prolong their lives, so they could repeat their mistakes and come back again. Was this what she was really meant to do with her life?

The rest of the day blurred in the routine of her shift. Amelia passed out meds, charted on her team of patients, and listened to her patient's list of ailments and complaints. That didn't include the endless phone calls to and from family members of the patients, doctors, and other departments in the hospital. It made for a long, hard day, leaving her exhausted and dreaming of tropical beaches and fruity drinks with tiny umbrellas.

Slowly maneuvering her computer cart down the hall, Amelia made her way to the nurse's station. Finding an empty spot out of everyone's way, she opened her charts. She could work and share a few laughs with the other nurses and unit secretaries, the closest she was going to get to a break or relaxing until the end of her shift.

"How does that sound to you, Amelia?"

She looked up, glasses sliding down the bridge of her nose.

"How does what sound?"

Piper grinned at her.

"It's Taco Tuesday. Unlimited Margaritas tonight." She gave Amelia a penetrating stare. "You've been ducking us for weeks now. Come on. You know you could use a night out. We won't stay out long. We all have to work tomorrow. But you know—tacos and margaritas!"

Amelia hesitated.

Piper glided across the nurse's station until she was standing in front of Amelia.

"Oh no, you don't! No excuses. You're coming with us."

She shook her head in resignation. "All right, but only one drink."

"It'll do you some good, honey." Bending over, Piper hugged her. "You know what they say about all work and no play."

Giving her a small smile, Amelia peered at the computer screen once again, focusing on the chart in front of her. It wasn't that she didn't want to go out with her friends. She loved them and enjoyed the camaraderie.

She'd been toying with the idea of changing jobs and wasn't ready to talk about it. Oh, she'd never give up nursing, but she wasn't sure Mason Regional Hospital was where she wanted to be anymore. Amelia had put out a few feelers and was waiting to hear back. She would decide when she had all the information in front of her.

A flurry of royal blue scrubs entered the double doors of the popular Mexican restaurant. Amelia's stress fell away as she made her way to the long table with her friends. Laughter and high-spirited chatter filled the air as they found their seats. The staff recognized them as regulars and hurried to fill their orders.

Amelia took a sip of the tart, iced drink, and the final weight of the day, knotted between her shoulder blades, fell away.

Piper winked at her from across the table.

"Better?"

She could only nod in agreement as she reached for a chip, dipping it in the bowl of salsa.

"I guess I really needed this."

"We all did," Layla piped in. "But you seem to have a lot going on right now. Care to share?" Her long blonde hair fell in waves around her shoulders rather than the tight ponytail she always wore at work. It made her appear younger, giving her heart-shaped face a delicate look.

Amelia bit at her lip. She should have known. Piper, Layla, and the others had gone through nursing school with her and knew her better than anyone, even her own sister. Of course, they would've figured out something was bothering her. She shrugged. If it was going to come out, it may as well be now. She stirred her drink as she tried to find the best way to drop the bombshell.

"I've been thinking of going agency."

That got their attention. The chatter abruptly came to a halt and five pairs of eyes locked onto her.

"You've been staff since you started. Did something happen?" Misty asked incredulously.

"You do not, how do you say it, make snap judgments," Dhanvi added. "You have been planning this for some time now, right?"

Amelia gave the Nepali nurse a sideways glance. She may stumble over the English language now and then, but she knew people and knew all of them quite well.

"Nothing is set in stone yet. I made a few calls, trying to see what's out there. All I know is I'm tired of what I'm doing. It's the same thing over and over. We get them better just so they can go out and do the same damn thing, bringing them right back to us." She threw up her hands. "I want to do something that makes me feel like I'm making a difference." She took a deep breath. "I was thinking of trying out hospice."

The nurses at the table quietly munched on chips and sipped at their drinks while they mulled over Amelia's words. Some of them had considered becoming travel nurses. Working for an agency gave them a much needed change of scenery, new people, new faces. It worked well for some.

"Call these people." Layla dug through her purse, pulling out a business card. "I talked to them not long ago. This may be what you have in mind."

"Thanks, I'll call them on my day off." Amelia picked up the small card. Guardian Hospice Agency was written across the front in gold lettering.

"Are you considering leaving us too?" Dhanvi gave Layla a shrewd look.

"I'm sure we've all considered leaving that floor if not the hospital completely." Thoughtful blue eyes scrutinized everyone at the table. "I'm not going to lie, I'd like to work somewhere not as stressful, maybe a clinic or private doctor's office. I just haven't found the right place yet."

Amelia glanced around. Every nurse at the table nodded in acknowledgment at Layla's words. Their jobs were hard. They all loved what they were doing, but there were days that were more of a struggle than rewarding.

"I didn't mean to drag you all down, but I'm glad to find out I'm not the only one who feels this way." She took a sip of her drink. "I'll call the agency in a few days. For now, we're in this together." Amelia lifted her glass to toast them. "Here's to nurses saving the world!"

Amelia closed the dryer door with the swing of a hip as she turned to pick up the laundry basket and gave a small sigh of relief. This was the last load and would get her through until her next days off. Amelia hated laundromats, but they went hand-in-hand with apartment living. Next time she moved, the apartment would come with hook-ups for a washer and a dryer, she promised herself.

She shifted the basket to one hip as she reached for the ringing cell phone in her back pocket. "Hello?"

"May I speak to Amelia Morgan?"

"This is she."

"Amelia, this is Sybil Browning. I'm with Guardian Hospice Agency. We spoke a few days ago. Did I catch you at a bad time?"

"No, not at all. I'm just doing laundry."

"We never get away from the mundane chores, do we?" The laugh was low and throaty. She didn't give Amelia a chance to respond, continuing on. "I have a job I believe is just what you're looking for. The patient is terminally ill with stage III cancer. She is transitioning to hospice and is set up for home care. The job is in Boothbay Harbor, Maine. You would have your own room and amenities, close to your patient. Five days on, two days off, and there will be a fill-in nurse on your days off. I can send you the information packet if you'd like."

"Yes, of course." Amelia swallowed hard. It was what she wanted, she just had no idea it would happen so quickly. Ending the call, Amelia slipped the phone into her back pocket. She guessed the old adage rang true. *Be careful what you wish for.*

There was nothing Amelia could do about the job or the offer until she got the information. Waiting wasn't her strong suit, but it didn't look like she had any option. Sitting down at her computer, she was surprised to see an email in her inbox from Guardian Hospice Agency. Opening the email, she scanned the note. Ms. Browning had emailed the packet to her, as well as mailed the information.

The patient was an eighty-seven-year-old female, Audrey Marchand. She had stage III cancer, and refused further treatment, opting for hospice care in her home, preferring to live her final days as she wished. A granddaughter and her husband lived with her. The granddaughter reached out to the agency for a full-time nurse because she needed help with the older woman. Audrey was non-compliant, being more than the younger woman could deal with.

Amelia twisted a long lock of chestnut hair around her finger. Well, she wouldn't be bored, that was for sure. Her patient was going to give her a run for her money. She glanced at the salary offered. It was quite a bit more than what she currently made. She had to make a decision quickly, though. If she accepted, they wanted her at the Marchand Cottage on Monday.

Amelia wrote a quick email, accepting the offer. Taking a deep breath, she hit the send button. She had some packing to do and arrangements to make. Better get busy.

CHAPTER 2

Amelia stared at the book in her lap, not seeing the words printed on the page. Most of the flight had been like that. She was nervous, seriously reconsidering her decision, although it was too late to back out. In the next thirty minutes she would be landing in Maine, where a man by the name of Robert Billings would pick her up and drive to her new job in Boothbay Harbor.

Stashing the book in her bag, she looked out the plane window at the overcast, dark, and gloomy sky. It didn't help her mood. She bit her thumbnail. Catching her reflection in the window, she yanked the offending digit from her lips. It'd taken her years to break the nasty habit, she wasn't going to start it up again now. Amelia took a deep breath—she would get through this, it was just nerves. She'd never traveled much, and this was a big jump out of her comfort zone.

The announcement to buckle up for landing came on, and Amelia mentally went through the next few steps—grab her carry-on, gather her bags, and find Robert Billings. Everything else would fall into place. She was here to take care of a hospice patient. The setting may be different, but it was still what she was trained for. She had this.

Thankfully, the landing was smooth. The tall passenger who had helped stow her carry-on appeared once again to aid her.

"Thank you, I appreciate your help." She gave him a grateful smile. "Being vertically challenged poses its own problems."

"We all have our own issues. Being tall can be hazardous, I've had to duck through more than one doorway." He laughed at his own joke. "Glad to be of service. Enjoy your trip." He gave a wink before turning to his own bag and departing the plane.

Cheered by the light-hearted encounter with her fellow passenger, Amelia made her way into the terminal, relieved to see a man holding a sign with her name. Walking up to him, she introduced herself.

"Hello, I'm Amelia Morgan."

"Hi there, I'm Robert Billings. Welcome to Boothbay Harbor." He shook her hand firmly, giving her a cheery smile. His brown eyes were large and friendly, reflecting his smile. "I guess I should clarify, we're not officially in Boothbay Harbor. It's a short drive to the actual town, and we live on the outskirts." He steered her toward the luggage carousel with a gentle hand at her back. "Let's get your bags, and we'll be on our way."

He never gave her a chance to speak, for which she was grateful. She'd never been good at small talk, but Robert was the friendly sort, putting her at ease quickly.

"Did you have a good flight?" Before she could answer the direct question, he was going on again. "Usually, the flights are smooth, but one never knows. Turbulence and all."

Robert didn't stop talking until her luggage was safely stowed away in the trunk of his sedan, and they were headed toward the cottage. He gave her a rueful smile.

"I suppose I should tell you, I'm in sales. It might explain why I tend to talk so much. Julia, my wife, constantly fusses about me not letting others get a word in edgewise." He shrugged helplessly. "What can I say? It's just the way I am."

"It doesn't bother me in the least. If anything, you've put me at ease." Amelia laughed lightly.

"Glad to hear it." He chuckled. "Now, why don't you tell me about yourself, Amelia? Why nursing? How long have you been at it? Is it everything you were looking for?"

His questions were shrewd in a disarming manner. After she'd answered, she had a feeling he knew more about her than people close to her. He must be one heck of a salesman.

"Look up ahead, Amelia. See that monstrosity? That's Marchand Cottage, where you'll be living for the immediate future."

"That's a cottage? And only three of you live there?" Amelia's jaw dropped. The place was huge! The size didn't make up for the state of disrepair, though. Patches of roofing were in need of repair, and the wood siding was in need of a coat or two of paint. The yard, while tidy, could have used some attention.

"This Tudor mansion was built in what was referred to as 'The Gilded Age.' Back then, these showcases were called cottages, probably because for the wealthy, they were summer homes." He shrugged at the simplified explanation. "Other than a small staff, it's just Audrey, my wife, Julia, and me."

Pulling up to the front, Robert parked the car and opened the trunk. Amelia picked up a smaller bag in addition to her carry-on. Robert continued speaking while they unloaded her luggage.

"The cottage holds fifteen bedrooms, twelve full baths, and two half-baths. As you can see, the house is not what it used to be. We've closed off most of the place because the upkeep is ridiculously expensive." Gathering her bags, he told her, "While Audrey's husband was 'old money' and provided quite well for his wife, I don't guess he took into consideration how expensive life would get or that his wife would live to such a rich old age." He lowered his voice as they approached the wooden double doors. "Frankly, when the old lady passes, I'm hoping I can convince Julia to sell this place and find something a bit more modest."

The doors opened, and an attractive brunette with a welcoming smile faced them.

"Welcome to Marchand Cottage, Amelia. I'm Julia. I hope my husband didn't talk your ear off on the drive up."

"Julia, that hurts!"

15

Amelia looked on in amusement. She could clearly see Robert's feelings weren't hurt, and the easy banter between them showed her how close they were. Robert reached Julia on the steps and gave her a tender kiss.

"I'll have you know, I didn't scare the woman off. She's right here!"

"Darling, she didn't have much of a choice. What was she supposed to do—throw herself from a moving vehicle?" Julia winked at Amelia. "Don't mind us. It takes a while to get used to our sense of humor. I promise you, it's all in fun." She rubbed her hands together. "Now, let's get you settled, and we'll introduce you to Grandmother."

Amelia followed the couple in, her neck straining as she tried to take in everything. The house may not be what it used to be, as Robert put it, but it was the most incredible home she'd ever seen. Beautiful antiques filled each room, and tasteful art decorated the walls. How many of them were originals? Going by what she'd seen already, she'd wager there were no copies in this home. She hurried to catch up while Robert and Julia waited for her at the bottom of the staircase.

"Sorry," Amelia said, blushing to her roots. "I've never seen anything like this before. It's beautiful."

"I'm glad you like it." Julia's face lit up at the praise. "I'll be happy to give you a tour once you're rested."

"That would be awesome. I'd love to see the whole house. Robert told me there are fifteen bedrooms. I can't imagine all that space." Amelia hoped she didn't sound like she was gushing, but she hadn't expected anything like this when Ms. Browning had filled her in on Audrey Marchand and her family.

Julia and Robert went past the stairway, down a wide hallway leading to several closed doors on each side.

"We moved Grandmother downstairs a couple of years ago. She was having trouble with the stairs, and we didn't want to take any chances with her falling. Her room is the first one on the right. We set up the room next to it for you. If there's anything you want changed, just let us know," Julia explained as they approached the room designated for Amelia.

Opening the door, Robert went in with her bags, depositing them by the side of the bed and gave her a warm smile. "I'll leave you with Julia to get settled and meet Grandmother Marchand. I need to run into town to pick up a few things for dinner tonight. You're not vegan, are you?"

"No, sir, I'm definitely a meat and potatoes kind of girl." Amelia grinned at the worried look on Robert's face. "Thank you for being so helpful. I appreciate it."

"It was my pleasure." He kissed his wife gently on the cheek. "Be back in a little while."

Julia walked over to a large closet. "You can hang your clothes here." She pointed at a large armoire against the far wall. "There should be enough drawers to store your foldables. There's an en suite, so you'll have all the privacy you need. I put fresh towels and linens in there. If there's anything else you need, let me know."

She faced Amelia with a wide smile.

"I'm sure the agency told you, but I want to make sure you're aware. We have a local nurse coming in on the weekends to relieve you. My car is at your disposal

17

if you want to venture into town. Boothbay Harbor is small, but there are quite a few shops and eateries you might find interesting. It's mainly a tourist town, so there aren't a lot who live here year round."

"Thank you. I'll take you up on your offer of the car. I'd love to go exploring. I'm a bit of a camera buff and would love to take pictures of the harbor." Amelia glanced around the room, making sure she had everything she would need. She couldn't wait to explore the expansive bedroom later, at leisure. Amelia was sure she could fit half of her apartment in this one room.

"It won't take me long to unpack. I figured I would be wearing my scrubs every day. What about meals? Does Mrs. Marchand dine with you, or does she prefer to eat in her room?"

"It depends entirely on how she's feeling that particular day." Julia gave her a helpless look. "When she feels well, we wheel her to eat with us in the dining room. On bad days, she stays in her room. You are more than welcome to eat with us. We dine at six-thirty."

"I guess I'll play it by ear for now. If it's all right with you, I'd like to change into my scrubs and meet Mrs. Marchand to give her a quick check, so I can start a routine."

"Of course," Julia agreed. "I'll wait for you in the hall. I have no doubt she heard us pass and is impatiently waiting for your appearance."

CHAPTER 3

A stern voice rebuked Amelia as she entered the room.

"Took your time about getting in here, considering I'm the reason you're here at all. Come closer so I can see you better."

Amelia blinked, stunned by her patient's abrupt manner. Sitting in a wingback chair next to her bed was an elderly woman, who no more looked like she was dying than Amelia herself. Audrey Marchand wore a stylish gray wig and a bold, red kimono. Amelia could see hints of blush on her cheeks and a light touch of lipstick on her pursed lips.

"Grandmother! Don't act so imperious. You'll scare your nurse away before you get a chance to be introduced," fussed Julia, nervously fluttering her hands before grabbing one of Amelia's, pulling her forward.

"I have two weeks to decide if I want to keep her as my nurse. You know I don't waste time. I'll make up my mind in the next thirty minutes." Audrey motioned for Amelia to step closer.

In her mind, Amelia rolled her eyes. She'd had patients like Audrey before and knew how to deal with them. The problem was before, she'd been able to leave the room and tend to other duties and patients. Here, there was no place to go.

"Good afternoon, Mrs. Marchand," said Amelia, stepping up and offering a hand. "I needed to unpack a few things I would need immediately. How are you feeling?"

The wrinkles around Audrey's mouth deepened as she pursed her lips together even more.

"I'm dying, girl. What more do you need?"

Amelia ignored the fact the elderly woman hadn't taken her hand. She raised a brow, tilting her head toward the bed.

"May I?" Amelia sat before the woman could answer. *Take that.*

Julia gasped, and Amelia chuckled inwardly. Things were getting ready to get real. Audrey harrumphed, then waved a hand at Julia.

"Go on, Julia, we'll be fine. If you'll be so kind as to bring in some tea for us, dear. I want to get to know my nurse."

Julia gave Amelia a worried look, but with a glance, Amelia let her know she could handle the situation. When the door closed behind the woman, Amelia turned back to Audrey.

"I understand from your granddaughter you have good days and bad days. Apparently, today is a good one. Do you sit in your chair often?"

It was as if the wind was taken from Audrey's sails. She faltered, then answered as she smoothed down her wrap.

"Most days, I don't have the energy to get up. I wanted to be presentable when you arrived."

Amelia smiled at the elderly woman. "I appreciate the gesture but would prefer if you were comfortable. Would you like to get back in your bed? We can chat while I get you settled."

With a small sigh, Audrey nodded. "That would be nice."

The next few minutes were spent getting the woman settled in her bed under the covers. Amelia chatted gaily, asking her about her daily routine and appetite, learning a lot in those few minutes. By the time Julia returned with their tea, Amelia was putting away the blood pressure cuff and stethoscope. Setting the tray on a dresser, Julia went about pouring cups of tea. Amelia sat in the chair vacated by Audrey.

When Audrey was served, she took a dainty sip and asked, "Amelia, tell me, dear, have you ever been in love?"

The question was so far out of left field, Amelia choked. Coughing, she tried to catch her breath and regain her composure.

Julia wore an odd smile.

"No, ma'am. I've never been in love. I've been too busy with school, then nursing, to get out much."

"You're young yet. I'm sure some dashing young gentleman will come around." The elderly woman gave her a faraway look. "I was in love once, very young at the time. This was before I met my George, you understand. Don't get me wrong. I cared for my husband, but he couldn't compare to my Alex."

Amelia shot a glance at Julia, praying for some kind of guidance. All she received for her trouble was the mouthed word '*later*.' Oh well, she was going to have to muddle through this the best she could and hope for answers later. She ran a nervous finger over the rim of her cup. Amelia needed to say something. She could tell from the way Audrey was looking at her some sort of response was expected.

Taking a deep breath, she blurted, "What happened that you didn't marry him instead?

By the smile on Audrey's face, Amelia had asked the right question. Julia wore a resigned look. Apparently, this was a familiar tale to the granddaughter.

"He refused to make me like him, so he left."

"Like him?" Amelia asked, confusion and a little bit of curiosity in her question.

Audrey smiled sadly. "Yes. You see, my Alex was a vampire."

Amelia's eyes widened in surprise. She hadn't seen that one coming. A chuckle came from the corner of the room.

"I'll explain everything over dinner," Julia told her. "For now, we've lost her. We best get her comfortable."

Alarmed at Julia's words, Amelia's startled gaze fell on Mrs. Marchand, and she jumped to her feet. The elderly woman's eyes held a vacant stare, and she wore a bemused smile.

"She's fine, Amelia. You'll get used to it," Julia explained. "The only thing keeping her going are her memories. Right now, she's lost in them. I think they give her comfort."

Julia went about putting away the teacups and together, they situated the patient as Audrey's eyes slowly closed, drifting off to sleep.

Amelia sat at the vanity, towel-drying her long, wavy hair. She still had time before dinner was served. Thankfully, she'd packed a few nice outfits in addition to her scrubs. In this household, she would need them.

She was curious about the coming conversation with Julia, the one that promised to enlighten her about Mrs. Marchand's story of Alex. Did the woman truly believe her first love was a vampire? If so, Amelia was unsure of how to proceed, other than to humor the old woman. Amelia didn't give credence to vampires and spooky things that went bump in the night. She was a see-it-to-believe-it kind of person. She didn't have time to waste on things that weren't real. Amelia sighed as she tossed the damp towel into a clothes hamper. This was definitely not what she'd expected when she'd accepted the position.

Amelia slowly walked toward the dining room. Even though she was curious about what Julia had to say, she didn't want to encourage ghost stories. She'd have to figure out what to do once she heard the whole tale. Robert and Julia were already seated when she entered the room. They gave her a welcoming smile, motioning for her to sit across from Julia while Robert sat at the head of the table. A young woman was silently filling their plates.

"How was your first day, Amelia? Not too daunting, I hope," Robert asked.

"Not at all, just getting settled in and meeting Mrs. Marchand," Amelia answered as she discreetly tried to inch her chair closer to the table.

"I hope Grandmother Marchand didn't overwhelm you." Robert gave her a worried look. "She can be a little stuffy at times."

Julia gave a small sigh. "She's already pulled her *'I'm the Queen, do my bidding'* act. Luckily for us, Amelia went with it and survived." She gave Amelia a searching stare. "She didn't scare you off, did she?"

"It's all good." Amelia lightly laughed as she unfolded the napkin and placed it on her lap. "Though I'll admit, she threw me off with her story about Alex."

Robert choked on his soup. Reaching for his napkin, he cast a furtive glance at his wife before speaking. "She told you about him? Already?"

"Grandmother has never kept it secret about her first love, Alexander. Everyone in the family has heard of him, though no one has ever seen or met him."

"If she loved him so deeply, why did she marry someone else?" Amelia asked, then tasted the steaming first course.

"According to the tale, after Alex left, Grandmother refused suitors for years, always hoping he'd return. Then Grandfather showed up. He knew the story of Alex but refused to let it hinder his pursuit of Grandmother's hand. When he told her he could never replace Alex in her heart but would spend a lifetime loving and taking care of her, she finally relented. My great-aunt Ophelia, Grandmother's sister, told me once, it was

Grandfather's promise that made her accept his proposal. She married him, raised a family together, and never spoke of Alex again."

Amelia pushed her plate away, her thoughts on the bittersweet story. "It's a heartbreaking story, but a vampire?" She questioned her hosts with a confused glance. "Where did that come from?"

"Grandmother would only say he was a creature of the night and left because he didn't have the heart to make her like him. He wanted her to have a normal life."

"I guess that makes sense,"—Amelia shuddered—"in a macabre fashion."

"We all feel the same way," Robert assured her. "No one has ever been able to convince Grandmother Marchand otherwise. Now, we just let her talk. Since she was diagnosed with cancer, she's been melancholy."

"I imagine it's only to be expected," Julia added.

"It is." Amelia gave the couple a sympathetic look. "Most elderly people take comfort in reliving happier moments as they near their time."

"She hasn't brought Alex up in quite a while. Do you think it means anything?" Julia asked, the worry plain on her face.

"There's no way of knowing for sure. He was her first love. I'm sure those memories bring her comfort." Pushing away from the table, Amelia excused herself. "Thank you for the delicious meal. I'm going to check on Mrs. Marchand before I turn in."

Robert smiled at her as Julia spoke, "Rest well, Amelia. If you need anything at all, we're down the opposite hall. We've always stayed close by in case Grandmother Marchand needed us."

"Thanks. I'll see you in the morning."

Making her way to Mrs. Marchand's room, Amelia hoped her patient would have a restful night.

It hadn't taken long to check on her patient. The elderly woman still slept peacefully, even while Amelia went through her routine. Preparing for bed, Amelia's gaze was drawn to streaks of lightning blazing across the night sky. As she drew closer to the window, the rumble of thunder grew louder. She shivered when her fingertips touched the cold glass. They were in for a stormy night. A flash of movement in the yard made her jump back. Squinting into the darkness, she tried to see what was out there—nothing. She didn't have an overactive imagination. Audrey's talk of vampires must still be in her mind.

Amelia pulled the heavy drapes shut and slipped between the cool sheets. Reaching out, she turned off the bedside light, settling in for the night. Her phone alarm was set to wake her periodically so she could check on her patient. It would do until she got used to her new routine. Hopefully, she could get some sort of rest in between.

Heart pounding and gasping for air, Amelia ran for her life—straight toward the woods. The wind whipped her long, thick hair into her face, blinding her as she fought desperately to get away from the manor house. Rocks tore at her bare feet as she struggled to keep her balance on the uneven ground. Her thin gown and wrapper were useless against the chill in the air.

Thunder reverberated in the sky as lightning strikes filled the air with an eerie light. As the storm gained momentum, so did the waves crashing against the cliffs.

26

Huge drops of cold rain pelted Amelia as she slipped and stumbled toward the safety of the trees.

Amelia sat up in bed, heart racing, her hand shaking as she pushed long locks from her face. Making her way to the bathroom, she squinted against the bright light as she flicked the switch. Standing in front of the lavatory, she waited for her vision to focus. A sheen of perspiration covered her face and chest.

As she studied her reflection, her thoughts went back to the dream—nightmare, really. She'd just started this job. Could the mere mention of a vampire trigger these reactions? Amelia had watched a million horror movies, but not a single one had ever caused her to have nightmares. Now this.

Looking down at her cami and shorts, the dream came rushing back. In it, she'd been wearing a long, flowing gown and sheer robe. Where had that come from? She never wore lingerie, always more comfortable in casual sleepwear. Running the water as she reached for a facecloth, she shrugged. It was just a dream. She was sure talk of Audrey's vampire boyfriend had triggered it, and the beginnings of the storm as she went to bed had probably added fuel to the fire. That was all. It was nothing.

After washing her face, Amelia raked her fingers through her hair into some semblance of order. Slipping on jeans and a shirt, she figured she'd check on Audrey while she was up. Maybe after that, she'd be able to sleep again.

Slipping quietly into Audrey's room, her patient tossed fitfully in bed. She guessed the storm was affecting the elderly woman's sleep too. The dim light from the bathroom cast enough light for Amelia to easily make her way to the bedside. Just as she reached Audrey, a peal of thunder reverberated, and a flash of lightning lit up the room. Startled, Amelia jumped at the sound, letting out a distressed squeak. The older woman sat straight up in bed, a hand clutching the neckline of her gown and looked directly at Amelia.

"Evil is coming. We must be on guard."

'Evil?' Amelia swallowed hard. First, vampires and now this. She had to admit it was beginning to creep her out. She sat on the edge of the bed next to Audrey, desperately trying to calm her own racing heart.

"It's just the storm. It probably gave you some bad dreams. Why don't we get you comfortable and I'll give you something to help you sleep." When she reached for Audrey, the woman caught her hands with a fierce grip.

"It's more than the storm, it's a sign."

"Mrs. Marchand, I'm sure everything will look differently in the morning. I'm going to get you a pill and a glass of water to help you get back to sleep."

As quickly as it had come on her, the fight went out of the woman. She laid back down, allowing Amelia to rearrange her covers. When her gaze met Amelia's, they were filled with sadness.

"I wish Alex was here. He would protect us."

Amelia had no response. She was in a strange house filled with strangers. She didn't know them or their history. Were they all mentally unstable, and she was stuck here, far from home, family, and friends? For the first time, Amelia found herself unsure of not only her surroundings, but of her decision to be here. It wasn't a good feeling.

CHAPTER 4

Amelia awoke to sunshine peeking through the cracks of the drapes and birdsong outside her window. Rising, she pulled the heavy curtains open and basked in the warmth through the glass. She needed to dress and check on Audrey, but after last night, she required a few moments of normalcy first. With a sigh, she turned to dress.

Running fingers through her long hair, she peered at her reflection. Amelia had never bothered with make-up except when she went out socially. Here was no different. While most nurses pulled their hair back into a ponytail or a messy bun, Amelia chose to wear hers down. Even though her hair was wavy to the point of curly, it never gave her any trouble if she wore it down. Pulling it back or pinning it guaranteed snarls she didn't have time for. She put on her glasses, which promptly slid down her nose. With a huff, she turned to leave the room. Amelia had contacts, but like make-up, never bothered with them. Her life was resigned to repeatedly pushing her glasses back in place throughout the day.

Tapping lightly on Audrey's door, the woman called out softly.

"Come in."

With a smile firmly in place, Amelia opened the door, happy to see Audrey appeared rested. Apparently, the night before hadn't left any lingering effects.

"Good morning, Mrs. Marchand. Were you able to get some rest last night?"

"After you gave me the pill, I did. Thank you. What about you? I imagine being in a strange place with a storm going on did nothing to help you sleep."

"I've had better first nights, but I did manage to get some sleep after I checked on you. Hopefully, today will be better for both of us." Amelia lightly laughed as she checked the woman's vitals, then checked the list on the dresser. Julia had written out Mrs. Marchand's daily routine. They agreed it was best for the patient if nothing changed too much in her everyday life. Audrey preferred to bathe before breakfast, a simple enough request. Gathering what she would need, Amelia made small talk as she prepared for her patient's bath.

"Do you have any idea what it looks like outside, my dear?"

"When I peeked outside my window, the sun was shining," Amelia answered gaily.

"Splendid." A satisfied smile slid into place on the older woman's face. "Please let Rachel know I'd like to breakfast on the patio." Doubt crept over her face for a moment. "You'll take me outside, won't you?"

Amelia gave her a winning smile. No doubt, the older woman got her way countless times with that beguiling look. "Of course, I will. Let me find Rachel then I'll step outside and see what the weather is like. You may need a light sweater if it's cool."

Happy with Amelia's answer, Audrey sat in her chair, bible in hand. "I'll just read while you get things ready."

"I won't be but a moment," Amelia assured her as she left the room to search for someone named Rachel.

Finding her turned out to be easy—she met Amelia in the hall rolling a small cart with breakfast for two. Giving her Mrs. Marchand's request, Amelia headed outside to check out the patio and weather. Finding the way with no problem, she was pleased to see the weather was sunny and warm, a drastic change from the night before. Her patient would enjoy her breakfast outside.

While Amelia helped her into the wheelchair, Mrs. Marchand didn't say a word, focusing on the job at hand, conserving her strength. Once she was situated in the chair, Amelia caught a soft moan and winced. Audrey acted as if she was stronger than she actually was. In reality, she was very frail. As Amelia carefully pushed the chair through the house, Audrey perked up the closer they got to the patio. Wheeling her through the back door, Audrey threw her head back, soaking up the warmth from the sun. There was no doubt about it, the woman loved being outdoors. Once they were settled and eating, Audrey pointed to a corner of the massive backyard.

"See the gazebo over there?"

Amelia looked up to see a beautiful wooden structure she'd somehow missed when they'd sat down.

"That's where Alex and I used to meet. We spent hours sitting and talking. He always came at twilight. As night deepened, he would point out the constellations and tell me stories about them."

Amelia pushed her plate away as she wiped her mouth with a linen napkin. The omelet had been delicious.

"How did you meet him?" she asked, figuring she could be polite without encouraging the vampire part of Audrey's story.

"My mother loved to hold parties. It didn't matter if they were small or large, she was happiest when she was planning something. The night I met Alex was a Halloween masquerade ball. There were no costumes, but everyone attending was required to wear a mask. I remember like it was yesterday."

"My mask was black and gold lace, a handmade work of art. I loved it so much and couldn't wait for the ball to wear it. Of course, I had to have a gown as stunning to match. Luckily, we had a woman who was a phenomenal seamstress. My mother would not hear of me wearing a black gown. At my age and unmarried, it just wasn't done. So, the seamstress designed a gown of gold. The skirt had panels of black lace that matched the mask perfectly. It was an exquisite outfit, and I knew I would outshine all the other girls there."

"In the South, where I'm from, you would have been the belle of the ball." Amelia couldn't help but smile at the woman's recollection.

Audrey smiled, the years melting from her face. At that moment, Amelia could easily see the beauty Audrey Marchand had been those many years ago.

"I like that," she murmured softly. "The belle of the ball..."

"So, tell me when you met Alex. Did you have to wait toward the end, or did he show up early?" By this time, Amelia was intrigued by the older woman's story, curious about the young lovers.

As a trembling hand struggled to lower the teacup without dropping it, Amelia helped her without making a fuss. She could see the woman's energy draining. The story of Alex would have to wait for another time.

"Let's get you back inside. I'm afraid this outing may have been too much for you." Amelia pushed her chair back and rose.

"Nonsense." Audrey's voice faltered. "I may be a little tired, though. A nap might be nice."

"Then that's what we'll do. Let's get you inside." Wheeling the chair from the table, she pushed her patient inside toward her bedroom.

Julia came around the corner, giving her a questioning look, mouthing, "Do you need help?"

Amelia shook her head to indicate she had everything under control. Once in the bedroom, it only took a few minutes to get Audrey into bed, and she was asleep almost instantly. Once she tidied up, Amelia looked around. While her patient slept, she didn't have much to do.

She suddenly remembered the paperbacks and puzzle books she'd thrown into her backpack in case she got bored on the flight over. She shrugged, now was

33

as good a time as any to finish the book she'd started on the flight over. Not much of a reader, she had nevertheless picked up a romance featuring a nurse as the main character, always meaning to read it. Now was her chance. Quietly slipping from Audrey's room to her own, she grabbed her laptop and backpack.

Returning to Audrey's room, she situated herself in a corner chair with a small end table, settling in for what she figured would be the first of many days like this one.

The door opened and Julia stepped inside. She peered around the room, her gaze settling on Amelia.

"There you are," she laughed.

Amelia stood and stretched her stiff back. How long had she been sitting in the chair? Glancing at her watch, she was shocked to see it was mid-afternoon.

Julia motioned toward her grandmother. "Has she been sleeping all day?"

"Pretty much," Amelia answered softly, walking to stand beside Julia. "She woke once, asking for something for pain. She refused lunch and went back to sleep. It's best if she rests.

"Why don't you take a break for a little while. I'll sit with Grandmother. No one expects you to sit 24/7 with her. Everyone needs time to themselves."

"Are you sure? I wouldn't mind stretching my legs for a little bit."

"I'm positive. The gardens are nice and if you want a longer walk, there's a trail in the back that leads up to the cliffs. The view up there is breathtaking." As if she remembered something, she added, "Stay clear of the woods, though. There are wild animals in there. I wouldn't want anything to happen to you."

Amelia grinned. "The cliffs sound perfect. There aren't any mountains or cliffs where I'm from. This will be a treat. I'll change clothes and get out there. I won't be long."

"Take your time." Julia chuckled low. "I have this."

With a wave, Amelia headed for her room. She'd been itching for the opportunity to explore, and now was her chance. She had a few hours before sunset, plenty of time to find her way up to the cliffs.

Once outside, Amelia took a deep breath as she looked around. With a little imagination, Amelia could envision what the gardens must have been like in their full glory, even though fall was quickly setting in. There were a few rose bushes still in bloom and other plants she had no knowledge of. They were pretty, though.

Aiming for the gazebo, she found the trail Julia had mentioned. She took a moment to stand in the covered structure, wondering what it had been like for Audrey to sit here, waiting for Alex to appear. She shook her head at her foolishness. Getting caught up in Audrey's story was totally unlike her, but this was a different place, different people. Everything here was totally unlike anything she'd ever known. Maybe it wasn't so strange entertaining these thoughts.

With a shrug, she pushed off the railing and started toward the trail. The dirt path mixed in with sand as she made her way up the steepening incline. She caught herself breathing a little harder, once again regretting turning down that gym membership. About half-way up, she paused to gaze out over the ocean. Sunlight sparkled over the cobalt waters as small, white-capped waves broke the surface, and seagulls cawed loudly as they flew overhead. The breeze picked up as she climbed higher. She was glad she'd grabbed a hoodie before leaving her room. Tied around her waist, she had a feeling she would need it when she reached the top.

When she approached the rocky height, Amelia gasped in astonishment. Whatever she'd been expecting when she got to the cliffs, it wasn't this. Off to her left were the woods she'd been warned about. Dark and thick with trees, the forest cast an ominous feel. They were a good distance off, so she figured she was safe. What caught her attention was the cemetery in front of the forest. Wrought iron fencing enclosed the crypts, and tall, iron gates kept them safe from intruders. Making her way toward them, the gate, while closed, wasn't locked. Chains hung from one of the gates with a padlock open through one of the links. The gate opened with a creak, telling her it had been some time since anyone had been here, no telltale tracks leading her to believe otherwise.

She carefully made her way around the crypts, noticing they were all above ground. There were no graves as she was used to seeing back home. She guessed the ground up here wasn't the best for digging. The dead were guarded better in their limestone and granite tombs. The names were faint but legible, and all were Marchands. The largest of the crypts sat prominently in the middle, a statue of a weeping angel sitting atop. The names Oliver and Sabrina Marchand were etched on the plaque with dates going back to the eighteen-hundreds. Counting the crypts, she surmised the Marchand's weren't a large family, or entire families were in each vault. Where would Audrey be laid to rest?

The clearing of a throat made Amelia whirl around. She battled to calm her pounding heart as she took in the sight of a tall, dark-haired man standing outside the gates of the small graveyard.

"I'm sorry. I didn't mean to startle you." He pointed toward the crypt she'd been looking at. "A family member of yours?"

"No." Amelia stood, shaking her head. "I walked up here and found this place. I was curious." *Why was she explaining herself to this man?* "Who are you?"

His smile was devastating. Even, pearly-white teeth were a perfect contrast to his olive complexion.

"Forgive me. My name is Demetrius Matteo. I come up here often on my walks. It soothes me to watch the waves from the cliffs. I couldn't help but notice you."

"Do you live around here?" She accepted his explanation. *At this point, what choice did she have?*

Once again, he flashed that smile. "I do." He pointed toward the woods. "I live on the other side. Do you have a name? I've told you mine. Fair is fair, after all."

Amelia couldn't help but return a smile. "Amelia Morgan. I'm working for the Marchand's."

"It's nice to meet you, Amelia." Instead of coming inside the cemetery grounds, Demetrius remained at the gate, hands gripping the iron rods. "I don't recall seeing you around before. Have you recently arrived?"

She nodded. "I'm a hospice nurse, caring for Mrs. Marchand."

Grief flashed across his face, and he turned to look at the ocean for a moment before returning his attention to her.

"I'm sorry to hear that. Audrey Marchand is a wonderful woman. The world will be a sadder place with her passing."

"You know her?"

Demetrius hesitated before answering. "I did, but it has been many years since I've seen her."

Amelia's brow furrowed at his words. He didn't appear that much older than her. How long could it have been? Oh well, it wasn't her business. Having seen all of the cemetery she cared to see, she made her way to the gate. When she got close enough, Demetrius opened it for her and walked with her toward the cliffs.

"Have you ever sat and watched the waves? I can spend hours up here."

"No, this is my first time to see the ocean."

He turned, motioning for her to join him. "Come sit with me, Amelia. We'll get to know each other while we enjoy the waves crashing below."

The old Amelia would have turned and run. But the new Amelia, the one who was encountering strange places and people, took a chance.

CHAPTER 5

As Amelia made her way carefully down the trail back to the manor house, her thoughts were filled with the dark-eyed, dark-haired Demetrius. Easy to talk to, he'd asked her questions about her life and she found herself answering him willingly. She'd never opened up to anyone like that before. He had an old-world charm she found appealing.

Even though she'd told him upfront she had little time and needed to get back to work, he took it in stride, making the most of the hour she gave him. He'd told her a little about himself, though keeping vague in some areas. He was from Greece, Athens specifically. His business was importing and exporting antiques, and he was here on a vacation of sorts, taking time for himself, leaving the business to his cousin and partner for a month or two.

Amelia had had a couple of boyfriends in high school, but never anything serious. Once she'd decided on becoming a nurse, she'd focused on her goal. What little social life she had was going out once in a while with her fellow nurses.

Demetrius was different. Amelia didn't know if it was because he was older or Greek, but she found him attractive and enjoyed talking to him. Would they cross paths again?

Hurrying inside the manor house, she went to her room to take a quick shower before slipping into her scrubs. She grabbed her things and made her way to her patient's room. Opening the door quietly, she found Julia sitting in the chair, reading a magazine while Audrey napped.

"Did you have a nice walk?" Julia asked, her friendly smile wiping away some of the stress from her pretty face.

"I did. I made it to the cliffs and watched the ocean. It was so relaxing." Audrey moved restlessly. Amelia figured she'd be waking soon. Her patient had been sleeping more often than not since she got there. Already speaking softly, she lowered her voice more, so as not to disturb the elderly woman. "I visited your family cemetery. I hope that was okay, the gates weren't locked. Some of the dates on the plaques are really old."

"Those gates haven't been locked in forever. No one goes up there anymore. Most of the plaques are very old," Julia agreed. "Almost our entire family is up there. There's a small mausoleum where my parents are. Grandmother will be laid to rest there as well. After Robert and I are buried, the vault will be filled. My son

40

is the last of my line. He won't want to be buried with the Marchand's."

Amelia's brow rose, but she didn't say anything. This was the first she'd heard of a son. Robert had never mentioned him, and while she'd seen several family pictures on the walls and end tables, she couldn't remember seeing pictures of Julia and Robert with a child. It wasn't her business, and she wasn't one to pry. Audrey stirred, catching Amelia's attention.

"Rachel will bring Grandmother's tray in an hour. You'll be joining us tonight?"

Amelia shook her head. "If you don't mind, I'll eat in here with Mrs. Marchand. She might need me tonight since she slept the day away."

With a nod of understanding, Julia left, closing the door behind her.

"What time is it, child?"

Turning back to her patient, Amelia answered softly, "Five-thirty, almost dinner time. Do you feel like eating a little? Julia will send us a tray."

"I probably should eat something," the older woman sighed. Frail and tired, she looked every bit of her eighty-seven years. "I just don't have much of an appetite today."

"Let's try to get down a few bites." Audrey gave her an apologetic look. "Maybe tomorrow, you'll have a better appetite." Gathering linens and towels, she gave her patient a sympathetic smile. As she helped Audrey to the bathroom to help her clean up, she asked, "Did you like sitting outside for your breakfast?"

"Yes, I truly did." Audrey's faded eyes lit up. "Do you think we could do it again in the morning?"

"I don't see why not," Amelia assured her. "As long as the weather is nice, it shouldn't be a problem."

"Did I hear right, you walked up to the cliffs?" Audrey slipped in as they were finishing her ablutions.

How much had the old woman heard while they thought she was sleeping?

"I did. Julia sat with you so I could stretch my legs for a little while."

"Not to worry, child." Audrey patted her hand, a rueful smile on her face. "Everyone needs a break. It has to be boring, watching an old woman sleep."

Laughing, Amelia shook her head, long waves shimmering around her shoulders.

"My job is never boring. I enjoy what I do, and I have books and a laptop when I have downtime."

"Still," Audrey persisted. "You need fresh air and exercise. When I was younger, I used to walk up to the cliffs all the time. I loved watching the waves ripple on still days and crash and churn when bad weather was coming. I've always loved the water." She sighed heavily. "After Alex left, I would spend hours up there, wondering where he'd gone to, what he was doing." Audrey tugged on her robe, straightening as much as she could manage. "I never did finish telling you how I met him."

"No, you were telling me about the mask and your gown," she answered, helping the elderly woman into the wheelchair. "We didn't get to that part."

Holding up a finger swollen with arthritis, she declared, "I'll tell you over dinner."

42

An hour later found Amelia seated at a small table for two situated in a corner of Audrey's bedroom. Rachel served their meal silently, leaving just as quietly as she'd entered.

Audrey pushed her food around on the plate. Trying to encourage her to eat, Amelia urged, "Why don't you tell me how you met Alex while you eat your dinner?" Amelia sampled the clam chowder. "This is delicious. You should try some."

Audrey's eyes lit up at the mention of her first love. If talking about him would get her to eat, Amelia would listen to stories all night.

"Alex was so handsome. I was waltzing with my uncle when I first saw him. He'd just entered the ballroom and I couldn't take my eyes off him. Splendid he was, all dressed in his finery. He was dark and dangerous looking, his hair and eyes as dark as the black tuxedo he wore." Her eyes took on a far-away look. "I'll never forget it. He was so striking. All the girls were simpering and flirting to get his attention as he made his way through the receiving line."

Caught up in Audrey's tale, Amelia was surprised to see Audrey had eaten half of the chowder before pushing it away. Maybe she was on to something.

"After the waltz finished, my uncle returned me to my parent's side. Alex was with them, and I was formally introduced. I was giddy with excitement but had been reared gently. A lady never let her emotions show." She actually winked at Amelia. "But, when he leaned over and kissed the top of my hand, I nearly swooned." Audrey's laugh was a little rough as if she hadn't done it in a long time. "Back in those days, a lady held a dance card, and gentlemen signed their names. Alex took my card and filled every line. He told me he fully intended to monopolize all my time to get to know me better. It was quite brazen, but I was young and taken with him."

Audrey raised a goblet of water to her lips, her hands not as shaky as the last time. She sat back in her chair, an amused smile playing on her lips, chuckled, then continued her story.

"Oh, we were the talk of the ball that night. All the girls were furious because they couldn't get close to Alex. We danced the night away. At one point, we stepped out for a breath of air. Alex had gone in search of champagne for us. When he returned, he toasted me, *To the most beautiful young woman at the ball tonight and the start of an amazing journey.*" Audrey smiled at the memory. "Of course, my foolish heart skipped a beat at his words." She eyed Amelia seriously. "He kept his word, though. Even though it didn't happen the way I wished, it *was* an amazing journey."

CHAPTER 6

Two weeks passed with Amelia settling into a routine. Thankfully, other than the first night, she'd had no more nightmares. Even Audrey was resting peacefully. No more ominous warnings of evil coming.

Amelia had managed to slip away to the cliffs a few times but hadn't seen Demetrius again. It was probably for the best. She wasn't there for romantic trysts, she had a job to do. Though, to be honest, there was a small pang of disappointment at his absence.

As had become their now-familiar pattern, Audrey would wake with a questioning look.

"It's a beautiful day. Breakfast on the patio," Amelia would answer with a smile. She didn't know what would happen when the weather turned too cold to eat outside. Audrey was never going to get better, but her mental alertness was so improved compared to when Amelia had first arrived. Of course, Amelia admitted, talking about Alex helped her immensely. Out on the patio, they were undisturbed, and Audrey was free to speak about her past.

Gathering clouds quickly moved across the sky. The wind had picked up with a nip in the air. Fall was moving in, and she was glad she'd picked a heavier sweater for Audrey. Amelia stilled—they were being watched. The hairs on her arms rose, and she rubbed them to ease the unsettling chill that suddenly filled her. She glanced around the yard but could see no one.

"Are you cold, child? We can go inside now."

"No, I'm fine. We can stay here as long as you like," Amelia reassured her.

The old woman pierced her with a shrewd look. "It's not the weather, what bothers you?"

"I'm not sure. For a moment, I felt like we were being watched, but there's no one here." Amelia didn't want to distress Audrey, but her patient had her faculties about her and wasn't a fool either.

Audrey surveyed the yard slowly, then tilted her head, listening. "Let's go inside, Amelia. I feel you are correct."

That was *so* not what she wanted to hear.

"Did you see someone?"

The elderly woman hesitated as she glanced around the yard once more.

"No, my eyesight is not what it used to be, but I sense something, and it's not good."

As Amelia wheeled Audrey back inside, she looked over her shoulder one last time. The wind had picked up even more and clouds now covered the sun, leaving a gray overcast to the sky which had been bright and sunny mere minutes before. She shivered, closing the door to the changing weather. Squaring her shoulders, she pushed her patient back to her bedroom.

Once she'd settled Audrey into bed, it didn't take long for her to drift back to sleep. As much as she enjoyed going outside, it took a toll on her. She usually slept most of the day. Audrey admitted to her once, it was easier to just sleep. When she was awake, she had to deal with cancer eating away at her and the pain it brought. Sleep was her haven. Studying the frail woman, Amelia let her sleep in peace. Cancer was a vicious monster that attacked without mercy, never leaving enough survivors. Audrey had lived a full life, but she still didn't deserve to die like this.

After tidying the room, Amelia settled in the comfy chair she now claimed as her own. Her books were stacked on a side table, along with a deck of cards. Julia had been teaching her how to play a few of her favorite games. While not her strong suit, Amelia had caught on to the nuances of the games, finding they were a good way to pass the time. As if she had summoned the woman, Julia peeked inside the room.

"Hey there, I was wondering if you wanted to take a break. I know it's not the best of weather, but you have a few hours before the rain comes."

Amelia didn't hesitate. "I'd love that. I'm going to braid my hair first. If I don't, I'll never get the snarls out. The wind was really kicking."

"It'll be stronger out on the cliffs. Just be careful on the trail. I don't want you blowing away."

"I'll be extra careful. See you in an hour."

47

Julia shook her head. "There's no rush, Amelia. Take your time."

Amelia was glad she'd packed her down jacket. Zipped and hooded, she trekked through the backyard to the trail leading to the cliffs. The sky was grayer, but there wasn't any sign of rain. Hopefully, the brewing storm would hold off for an hour or two. Amelia patted her chest, assured her camera was there. She wanted to take pictures of the ocean while the water was rough and choppy, forming small whitecaps on the surface.

It took her a little longer than usual to reach the cliffs. The wind had proved a challenge, buffeting her frame along the trail. By the time she reached the top, her lungs were burning from the exertion. Easing to the edge, she sat down and pulled her camera out, adjusting the settings. Engrossed in capturing the waves below, she didn't hear him until he was right behind her.

"Amelia, I didn't expect to see you out here today."

Startled, she almost dropped her camera over the edge. Demetrius caught it and handed it back to her, sitting down beside her.

"I'm sorry. I didn't mean to startle you."

She swallowed hard, trying to gather her scattered wits.

"I didn't hear you, and thanks for catching my camera. I'd hate to have to replace it."

His smile was every bit as alluring as she'd remembered, and he had dimples when he smiled, she hadn't noticed them before.

"Is photography a hobby of yours?"

"Sort of." She nodded, and the hood fell back, her long braid working its way out of her jacket. "I want to take a class on photography, but I never find the time."

"You know what they say about all work, Amelia." Demetrius' eyes danced with amusement.

She shrugged. "I know, but twelve-hour shifts working at a hospital don't give a lot of leeway to take courses."

"But you don't work at a hospital anymore." Demetrius wrapped his arms around his knees as he watched the waves. "Perhaps you could find the time now." He looked over at her. "There's more to life than work."

Amelia drew a pattern in the loose sand with a stalk of dried grass.

"What is wrong, Amelia?" Demetrius covered her hand with his, stopping her movement.

"Nothing. Why do you ask?" She pulled her hand back, dusting the sand from her fingers.

"Something is bothering you." Demetrius studied her carefully. "You seem distracted."

She sighed softly. "I guess I'm more unsettled than anything else."

"Would you like to talk about it?" He added with a soft smile, "I'm a good listener."

"It's probably nothing..." Amelia managed a tremulous smile.

Demetrius reached for her hand, linking their fingers together.

"Talk to me, *mikros*."

Taking a deep breath, then exhaling slowly, Amelia told him of her nightmare the first night and of Audrey's dire warning. She finished with this morning's eerie feeling of being watched and once again, Audrey's agreement.

"I just feel something is going to happen, and it's going to be bad. It's got me jumpy. The fact Audrey feels the same way is adding fuel to the fire."

"Sometimes," Demetrius spoke hesitantly, weighing his words, "it's good to listen to that inner voice or feeling. The fact you've had two experiences and Audrey has had similar feelings tells me you are probably correct. Is there someone in the household who makes you uneasy?"

"No, not at all. There are only a handful of staff, and Robert and Julia. Everyone has been very nice, and no one has hit the creep factor."

Demetrius chuckled low, the timbre of his voice encasing her with warmth.

"You should trust your creep factor." He stood, pulling her up with him. "Allow me to escort you back to the manor."

"You don't have to do that." The flush heat her cheeks, even though a cold wind was whipping around them.

"I would feel better, knowing you reached your destination safely. It would be my pleasure."

Gazing into his dark, liquid eyes, Amelia felt safe. She was glad he was with her.

Before he left her at the gazebo, he caught her hand.

"You are off on weekends, correct?" At her nod, he continued, "Go out with me Saturday night. There's a small tavern in town. I'll take you to dinner." Amelia

50

hesitated and Demetrius tugged on her hand. "Say yes, Amelia. I want to spend more time with you."

She couldn't resist his smile, or him.

"Yes, I'll go out with you Saturday night."

He kissed her cheek lightly. "I will be at the front door at seven."

"Seven," she echoed. Turning to make her way to the house, she couldn't peel the smile from her face.

She had a date.

CHAPTER 7

Seated at the dinner table, Amelia listened to Robert describe two co-workers arguing over the last doughnut left in the breakroom. The man definitely had a way with words; Amelia could picture the scene vividly. She and Julia were laughing so hard by the end of his story they both had tears streaming down their cheeks.

The ringing of the doorbell was foreign in the manor home, and everyone stilled at the sound. Robert stood, dropping his napkin onto the table.

"I'll see who it is."

Amelia could hear him conversing with whoever was at the door, but she couldn't make out the words. A few minutes later, he returned, a young man at his side.

"Julia, look who has returned home."

Amelia and Julia turned at the same time. Julia gasped, knocking over her water goblet as she rose.

Amelia quickly picked up the glass, placing napkins over the spill.

"I have it," Amelia murmured as Julia stood frozen in place.

Julia gave her a nervous smile, then stepped forward to greet the newcomer.

"Geoffrey, why didn't you call to let me know you were coming?"

She reached out to hug him, but Geoffrey clasped her hands instead, holding her at arm's length.

"You know me, Mother, I wanted it to be a surprise."

"When did you get..." The words were lost as she cleared her throat. "How long will you be staying?" There was palpable tension in the interaction between mother and son.

Pulling out a chair, Geoffrey sat across from Amelia. Ignoring his mother's question, he stated, "I see I'm in time for dinner. I hope there's some left."

Julia blanched. "I'll check in the kitchen. I'm sure there's plenty."

Robert took his seat, his lips in a tight line.

Geoffrey's gaze landed on Amelia. "And who do we have here?"

Robert coughed, then answered, "This is Amelia Morgan. She's Grandmother Marchand's hospice nurse."

Amelia met his gaze, offering a polite, "Nice to meet you."

Cold gray eyes met her own. Exposed to his glacial stare, Amelia took an instant dislike to him. Usually a good judge of character, she had a feeling she wasn't going to be wrong about this one.

"Polite little thing, aren't you?"

Geoffrey undressed her with his eyes, and Amelia couldn't help but shiver under his scrutiny.

He turned his attention to Robert. "So, Gran is finally ready to kick the bucket? It's about time."

Amelia almost choked at Geoffrey's words. *Who did that?* It was official, she didn't like this guy. It didn't matter how much she liked and respected his parents, she wanted nothing to do with him.

"Geoffrey!" Julia's voice was stern, but the reprimand fell on deaf ears.

"Oh please, Mother, the old woman is nearing one hundred if she's a day. It's time to move on. Has her will been updated?"

With a shaky sigh, Julia sat at the table. Robert squeezed her hand, and an unspoken communication passed between them. There was a lot of drama going on, and Amelia was very uncomfortable but couldn't find a graceful way to leave the situation.

"That will be enough of that kind of talk, Geoffrey. You're upsetting your mother," Robert admonished.

Geoffrey raised a brow, sending Robert a sardonic look.

"Still trying to protect Mother dearest? I guess it keeps a comfortable roof over your head."

"Geoffrey, enough! You haven't been here ten minutes, and you're already causing strife. If you can't behave, I'm going to ask you to leave," Julia exclaimed, staring defiantly at her son. The woman's hands trembled before she placed them in her lap, out of sight. A brave front, but it had cost her.

The young man waved a hand at his mother. "This is my home, too, Mother, in case you've forgotten." His

54

lecherous gaze fell on Amelia. "I think I'm going to stay awhile. It might prove interesting."

Amelia squirmed under his gaze. She'd had enough of his rudeness and innuendos. There was no way she was going to sit at the table and make herself a target for his gibes. Excusing herself, she hurried from the room. The pretext of checking on Audrey was legitimate, but it had sounded weak, even to her ears.

Softly closing the door behind her, Amelia leaned against the solid wood. Eyes closed, she tried to regulate her breathing and get her emotions under control. At least in here, she didn't have to deal with Geoffrey's rudeness.

"What has upset you, child?" the frail voice from the bed called out to her.

"Geoffrey is here." Try as she might, Amelia couldn't control the quaver in her voice.

Audrey sighed. "You must stay away from him. He's nothing but trouble."

Swallowing hard, Amelia agreed one hundred percent with her patient. She would go out of her way to avoid him.

Amelia spent the next few days slipping quietly between her and Audrey's rooms, taking her meals with her patient. Fortunately, Geoffrey's arrival heralded unrelenting storms, so it was easy enough to remain in the two rooms.

Julia briefly visited with her, making sure she wanted for nothing. She never brought up the subject of her son or how they were faring with his sudden appearance. The whole affair was rife with suspicion and mystery, but Amelia wasn't the type to pry. There were some things one didn't need to know. If Julia or Robert chose to fill her in, that was another matter.

Instead she focused on Audrey, making sure she was comfortable as possible, listening to her talk about Alex, which ensured her eating. She asked the question that always stayed on her mind.

"Ms. Audrey, how did you find out Alex was a vampire?"

The older woman's eyes lit up.

Amelia smiled to herself, this was going to be interesting.

"We had been dating for several months, but only dinner dates in the evening, never during the day. He told me his business kept him busy, and I never questioned him further." She sat back against the stack of pillows as she gathered her thoughts. "One day. there was some function or other at the cottage. Of course, Alex gave his regrets, but Father was having none of it. He demanded to know why Alex never came around during the day. When I tried to explain it was because of his business dealings, Father pointed out it was Sunday. After that, I began to question Alex about his whereabouts."

"He just came out and told you he was a vampire?" Amelia asked incredulously.

"Oh my, no." Audrey laughed softly. "The conversation took most of an evening. I was terrified when he showed me his fangs, but I believed him."

"Did he bite you?" The shock showed on her face. This was not some old woman's fantasy, Audrey

Marchand was telling her the truth as she knew it. The look of sadness on her patient's face tore at Amelia's heart.

"No," she whispered. "It was then he told me he would never turn me. I deserved better than the only life he could give me. He insisted I live a normal life, marry a good man, and have a family. I pleaded with him, but he was firm. Not long after, he left. I never saw him again."

Amelia found herself growing attached to the older woman. It was impossible to keep a professional distance when the situation had them so close together.

Audrey's stories weren't always about Alex. She spent hours telling Amelia of her days as a young woman, growing up in an elite, genteel society. It was so different from today and how Amelia grew up. She hung on every word, finding herself fascinated. Amelia looked forward to times when Audrey felt good because then the stories would come.

It was after one of those stories, Amelia found herself humming happily to herself as she loaded the dinner plates on the small rolling cart Rachel had yet to come by to get. Amelia figured the maid must be busy, so she would help by taking it back to the kitchen.

As Amelia carefully backed out the room, she was focused on shutting the door rather than the cart in the hall. Pushing the cart met resistance. Looking up, she found Geoffrey smiling down at her, his hands holding the cart in place.

"Why haven't you dined with us, Amelia? I can't get to know you if you're never around."

Her breath caught, realizing she was essentially boxed into a corner with no way out.

"I'm not here to socialize. I'm here to care for your great-grandmother." Without meaning to, her voice came out haughty and disdainful. This guy brought out the worst in her and this was only the second time she'd seen him!

"Spirited, too." He rubbed his chin as he stared at her thoughtfully.

Before he could say more, Amelia pulled the cart free from his grasp. She'd show him *spirited*.

"Excuse me, I need to take this to the kitchen and return to Mrs. Marchand. It's almost time for her meds."

He placed a hand on the small of her back, leaning closer to her ear.

"Maybe then you can come out and play."

"I told you, I'm here to work. Now, if you'll excuse me."

His laugh, the sound discordant to Amelia's ears, followed her all the way to the kitchen. Her new job had just taken on a new level of difficulty, one she was going to have trouble dealing with.

CHAPTER 8

Amelia borrowed Julia's car to go to the quaint little town to pick up a few items she needed. The sun was shining brightly despite a chill in the air. Finding a radio station she liked, she cranked the volume up as she zipped down the road. She was glad there was little traffic because her mind was already shopping.

She wanted to peek into a couple of dress shops she'd found on previous trips to town. Tonight, she was going out with Demetrius and she wanted something pretty to wear. She'd packed a couple of dresses that would work, but it wouldn't hurt to shop around either.

Boothbay Harbor was a small community with a big harbor. Yachting and tourism kept it going in the summer, but things slowed to a crawl in the fall and winter. Amelia was perfectly happy with the lack of crowds, taking her time, browsing through the small shops. People were friendly and more than willing to help her find what she was looking for. At the third shop, she hit pay dirt—a dark, purple sheath that hugged her curves and sinful silver heels to complete the outfit. Staring at her reflection, she was amazed at the transformation a simple dress could make. But there was nothing simple about this dress. It was designed to be an eye-catcher. Amelia had never owned such a garment, until now. She was ready for Demetrius and their first date.

Emerging from the dress shop, Amelia's stomach rumbled as she glanced at her watch. No wonder her stomach protested, it was past her usual lunchtime. Making her way across the road, she headed for a small diner.

Chatting with the waitress, she ordered a cheeseburger and fries. Waiting for her meal, she stared out the large front window, taking in the view of the town. It was a quaint little place with neatly tended storefronts in different colors with brightly painted signs. It was unlike any town she'd ever seen. Of course, Amelia amended her thoughts, it wasn't like she'd traveled a lot before either. Seeing the charm of this small harbor town found her wanting to discover others like it. She made a promise to herself to travel when she could.

After lunch, she took her time returning to the cottage. She'd thoroughly enjoyed her shopping spree and was looking forward to more trips into town. Its picturesque scenery would keep her captivated for longer than she would probably stay. She would take advantage of the situation and give her camera a serious workout.

Once back in her room, Amelia still had plenty of time to get ready for her date. She indulged herself by polishing her nails and playing with different hairstyles, though in the end, she wore her long, curly hair down. Elaborate hair styles just weren't her, and she wasn't going to pretend otherwise.

Slipping on the sexy heels, she admired her reflection in the mirror. The dress was flattering to her curvy shape, and the heels gave her diminutive stature some much-needed height. The outfit was an ego booster, and she didn't regret a dime she'd paid.

A light tap on her bedroom door caught her attention. Opening the door, she found the maid, Rachel.

"There's a gentleman at the door for you, Miss Amelia."

"I'll be right there." Amelia nervously smoothed down her dress. "I just need to grab my purse. Thank you, Rachel."

One last look in the cheval mirror gave her a boost of confidence. Picking up her coat and purse, she followed the maid from her room.

One glimpse at Demetrius as Amelia closed the door behind her had her insides clenching. The man looked as if he'd stepped from the pages of GQ magazine. All in black, his tie was the only spot of color, the exact shade of purple as her dress. His dark eyes took her in, his smile gleaming against his olive skin.

Taking her hand, he kissed it lightly. "You are breathtaking, Amelia."

Feeling the heat rush to her cheeks, she stammered, "Thank you," not trusting herself to say anything else. It would have come out cheesy, and she wanted to impress him, not make an idiot of herself. Amelia inwardly rolled her eyes. Where did that come from? She'd never tried to impress a guy before, why this one? One look at his lean, muscular frame as he opened the car door for her gave her at least one reason. The guy was hot! They didn't have men like this where she came from.

Settling into the passenger seat of his luxury sedan, Amelia had a feeling this was going to be a very special night.

They parked in front of a small restaurant Amelia had seen earlier. Escorting her to the building, seated at their table, going over the menu and ordering, Demetrius was the perfect gentleman, his manners impeccable. He either ignored or never noticed the other female patrons eyeing him boldly. Amelia did, though, which made her feel all the more special for his undivided attention.

Their meal was unhurried, and conversation never lagged.

"Did you not like the food?" Looking down at her plate, she'd eaten almost everything. His was virtually untouched.

He waved a hand over the plate. "I never eat much. I wanted to spend time with you and show you a nice evening." Demetrius finished his glass of wine and covered his plate with a linen napkin. "Enjoy your meal. We are in no hurry." He glanced at the waiter, then back at Amelia. "Would you care for dessert?"

Amelia carefully wiped her mouth with the pristine napkin. "Oh, there's no way I can manage dessert." Shaking her head, she smiled ruefully. "The meal was heavenly, but I really am full."

Demetrius slipped the waiter a credit card, then turned back to Amelia.

"Would you like to take a walk on the wharf? I don't think it's too cold out, and the night is lovely."

"It sounds nice."

Helping Amelia into her coat, Demetrius draped an arm casually around her shoulder as they left the restaurant. Once outside, he linked his hand with hers, leading the way toward the wharf.

Standing on the wooden planks, they stared at the inky sky dotted with sparkling diamond-like stars. Demetrius once again draped an arm around her, pulling her closer to his side.

"Are you warm enough?"

Amelia wound an arm around his waist, marveling once again at his lean, muscular body. Looking up at him, she smiled.

"I'm fine, thanks." She peered up into the sky again. "I don't think I've ever seen so many stars before."

"Artificial lights from the cities are obscuring our view of the stars. It's a sad fact. Man is ruining a lot of natural beauty."

"True enough." Amelia sighed softly. "I'd like to see more of the world's natural wonders. I want to travel more."

"What's stopping you?" Demetrius' voice was a hushed whisper.

"Nothing. Everything. I guess I'm just now figuring out what I want in my life. I've spent all my time focusing on nursing school, then working." She glanced up to find him studying her intently. "I'd like to take some time to travel, you know, see the world."

"I have no doubt you will take the world by storm, *agápi mou*." He kissed the top of her head. "I would like to show you Greece. My country has a rich culture. I think you would enjoy it."

"It's on my bucket list," she admitted. "Maybe one day."

"One day, indeed."

A cool breeze picked up, causing Amelia to shiver despite her wool coat and Demetrius holding her.

"Let's head back to the car. I can't have you getting sick."

Amelia wasn't going to argue. It was getting noticeably colder this close to the water, and she wasn't dressed to brave the elements.

Once in the car, Demetrius turned the heater on, the warm air rushing through the vents. Holding her hands up against the slots, she relished the warmth.

"I am so sorry, Amelia. I fear we were out too long."

"No, no, I'm fine." She turned to face him. The only illumination in the car was from the dash, but she could see the concern in his face. Amelia reached out, placing her hand on his arm. "I enjoyed our evening. I didn't want it to end."

Pulling into the drive of the Marchand cottage, Demetrius killed the engine. He held her hands, squeezing them gently.

"I didn't want our evening to end, either. I also plan on this being the first of many, if you will accept."

The familiar flush creeping into her face again, Amelia was grateful the dimness would hide the telltale blush.

"I'd like that."

His smile widened at her words.

"As much as I would like to sit here and continue our conversation, it would probably be better if you went inside. I don't want to cause any problems with your employers."

"You're probably right." She fumbled for the door latch, but he stopped her.

"I'll get your door."

In a flash, Demetrius escorted her from the car to the door. A kiss on the cheek, a promise to see her soon, and he was gone.

Looking around, Amelia found herself alone. Heaving a soft sigh of relief, she hurried to her room. Once inside the safety of her bedroom, she leaned against the closed door. Her time with Demetrius had been precious, and she wanted to be able to play it back in her mind before sleep.

She couldn't wait to see him again.

Demetrius drove away feeling extremely satisfied with the way the evening had gone. Time spent with Amelia was worth every precious second. She was an enigma, innocent yet with a depth he'd never encountered before. It was an intriguing combination. He would have to tread carefully, though it hadn't stopped him from asking her for a date. A date, of all things! He couldn't remember the last time he'd asked a woman out. Then again, he couldn't remember the last time a woman caught his attention the way Amelia did.

There was something incredibly special about this particular woman and he found himself wanting to know her better, much better. It would all come in time, he would make sure of it. For now, he would take things slow. If needed, thinking back to their last conversation on the cliffs, he would take on the role of her protector.

Deciding not to go home immediately, Demetrius raced down the empty highway, allowing his mind to wander, something he ordinarily never did. He wanted to replay this evening, Amelia's bright blue eyes and hesitant smile blazoned in his memory. She'd gotten under his skin and he found the feeling comforting, much to his surprise.

CHAPTER 9

Now more than ever, Amelia eagerly anticipated her hour or two on the cliffs. Some days, Demetrius would show up, and they spent the time talking about everything under the sun. Other days, she would photograph the scenery around her or read. She only totally relaxed when she was away from the manor house.

With Demetrius, she could be herself. He made her laugh, forgetting the tension that now lived in the Marchand household.

As if her thoughts had summoned him, Amelia looked through her viewfinder to see Demetrius walking from the woods toward her. She pressed the shutter button, capturing his image. Amelia chided herself for her whimsy, but she didn't delete the pictures.

She smiled up at him as he drew closer. Today, he wore a lined jacket, dark jeans, and hiking boots. His hair was unruly and windblown, looking incredibly sexy.

"Amelia! I was hoping I would find you here, though with the weather, I had my doubts."

The past week or so had brought more than a fair share of thunderstorms but they'd abated, only to bring in a cold front. Once again, she was glad she'd researched the weather clime for Maine.

"Unless snow comes, I think I can deal with the weather," she laughed. Pulling gloves from her pockets, she waved them. "I just can't handle my camera easily with these."

He eased down next to her. Capturing her hands, he blew warm air on her fingers.

"Your fingers are like ice, you should wear your gloves. I'm sure it's too overcast to take good pictures, anyway."

"You're probably right." Amelia laughingly agreed with him. Even though she agreed, she wasn't ready to pull free of his touch. When he did let go, allowing her to put her gloves on, there was a pang of loss and disappointment. She enjoyed his touch, finding herself wanting more.

Demetrius draped a strong arm across her shoulders, pulling her closer. Snuggling against his hard frame, she inhaled his fresh scent that blended with the outdoors, fir trees and the tangy salt in the air.

"Is that better? Are you warm enough?" His voice was husky in her ear.

"Mmm, perfect," Amelia responded. And she told the truth. This moment in time was indeed perfect. Somehow the universe sent her someone she didn't realize she wanted or needed. Demetrius was inching his way into her heart and Amelia didn't want it to stop.

When he tipped her face to meet his, Amelia stared into dark eyes, liquid with emotion. His full lips were soft, his kiss tentative. Demetrius lightly nipped at her bottom lip, and she parted them, allowing his tongue access. Pulling her closer into his embrace, he deepened the kiss. Amelia fisted his coat, wanting more... and Demetrius obliged. When the kiss ended, she found herself lying on the ground, Demetrius propped on an elbow above her, caressing her face. Breathing heavily, all she could do was stare into his heated gaze. So, this was what the fuss was all about. She'd never been kissed like that.

"I've been wanting to kiss you for a while now," Demetrius offered.

Sitting up, Amelia attempted to dust herself off and looked at him curiously.

"We haven't known each other very long. Exactly what is *a while?*"

"I guess you have me there." Demetrius chuckled. "The moment I saw you, I wanted to taste your lips. You're quite beautiful, you know."

She ducked her head, feeling the heat flare in her cheeks.

"Amelia, has no one ever told you how attractive you are?"

"No," she admitted, shaking her head. "The guys I've dated weren't big on compliments."

"They were fools," Demetrius exclaimed. Pulling her back into his embrace, he whispered, "I would spend every waking moment telling you how beautiful you are, showing you how much you mean to me."

Amelia stiffened, and Demetrius released her.

"I'm sorry if I offended you. I know it's too much, too soon—but I've not lied to you either."

Hugging her knees, she stared out at the rough seas.

"This is moving too fast for me. I didn't come here looking for romance."

"But you found it, regardless."

"Did I?" Amelia met his serious gaze. "Or is this just a fling to occupy your time while you're here?"

His expression hardened at her words.

"Perhaps this *is* moving too fast, I'll give you that much. If you truly knew me, you would never doubt my words. I'm not like the other men you've known, Amelia. If you take the time to get to know me, you will discover it on your own." He held up a hand at her oncoming protest. "I know you're only here for a short time, and you take your job seriously. It doesn't mean arrangements can't be made when your time is up."

Picking up her gloved hand, he kissed her fingers. Amelia swore she could feel the heat through the thick material.

"I'm at liberty to travel and call home wherever I settle. I want to know you better, Amelia. I want to see if we can have a future together." He rose, pulling her up with him. "Don't say anything right now. Think about it. For now, let me walk you home."

Amelia was stunned into silence. Luckily, Demetrius kept up the small talk until they reached the gazebo.

Kissing her lightly, he pressed a small piece of paper in her hand.

"This is my cell phone number," he whispered into her ear. "Please let me know when you'll be at the cliffs again. Right now, it's the only time I have with you."

She searched his eyes. Finding nothing but an earnest plea, she nodded.

"Promise?"

"I will, Demetrius. I promise."

Another kiss and he was gone. Amelia watched him disappear down the path, her fingers pressed against her lips, sealing his kiss to her heart. Her thoughts were as jumbled as her heart was in turmoil. This was all new to her. She had a lot of thinking to do before she saw Demetrius again.

Turning toward the cottage, movement at one of the upstairs windows caught her attention. Staring upward, the drape slowly closed. Was someone watching her? With an uneasy feeling, she made her way inside. She needed to change and check on Ms. Audrey. She didn't have time for mysteries.

Amelia peeked in on Audrey on her way to her room. To her surprise, Audrey was awake and sitting up, talking quietly to Julia. Audrey waved a frail hand at Amelia as Julia rose to meet her at the door.

"Did you enjoy your walk? It seems to have done you well. There's color in your cheeks."

"I did. Though it was rather cold out." Amelia didn't know if the color was from the cold wind or the

71

lingering effect of Demetrius' kisses. Either way, she wasn't ready to share that little detail. "Can you give me a few minutes to change?"

"Of course. Take your time. Grandmother is feeling better today. I was going to check on her dinner tray. Will you be eating in with her again tonight?"

Pulling her braid free, she nodded, "I think it's for the best. Especially if Mrs. Marchand is feeling talkative."

Julia reached out, touching Amelia's arm.

"I'm sorry about Geoffrey." Her face tightened as she spoke about her son. "He's... very troubled. I understand you not wanting to be around him."

Amelia never intended to hurt the woman's feelings, it was the last thing she wanted, but Julia had hit the nail on the head.

Forcing a smile, Julia reassured Amelia, "I'll have to tell you that sordid story sooner rather than later, but not tonight. Let me see to your trays."

Before she could say anything, Julia had slipped down the hall. There was so much more to that story, but it was Julia's tale to tell. Amelia would just have to wait until Julia was ready to tell her. Peeking in at Audrey, Amelia smiled brightly.

"I'll be right back, I just need to change clothes. Will you be all right?"

"Take your time, child." The old woman nodded, waving her on.

Closing the door quietly behind her, Amelia smiled to herself. Her patient's attitude had done a complete turnaround in a short time. Audrey didn't give her a hard time about anything, which made her job all the easier.

Changing into her scrubs, Amelia stared at her reflection as she ran a brush through her long hair. She was surprised to see a rosy glow still in her cheeks. There was no way she could still blame it on the cold weather. She smiled softly as a wave of pleasure ran through her. Their talks were showing a side of Demetrius she wanted to know better. Was there a chance of building a relationship with him?

Braiding her hair, she forced her thoughts away from the sexy, dark-haired man, focusing instead on her patient. Audrey was her priority. The elderly woman was having a good day and Amelia wanted to make it last as long as possible.

Setting the brush down, she growled at her reflection. *I finally meet a wonderful man and I don't have time to give him. Life just isn't fair.* Of course, Amelia already knew that.

Audrey smiled sweetly at her as Amelia entered the room. Rachel was setting up her tray and Amelia stepped in to make her patient comfortable. It didn't take long before they were both seated and eating their dinner.

"Julia tells me you've been walking up to the cliffs. Is there something special up there that keeps you going back?"

Amelia fought to keep her emotions in check. She didn't want anyone to know about Demetrius. The last thing she wanted was to be accused of dereliction of duty. Her entire life revolved around nursing. She didn't want to mess up on her first assignment as a travel nurse.

"I love photography." It was the safest way to answer Audrey's question. It was the truth, just not the whole of it. "I've never seen a landscape like the one here, and I spend my time taking pictures of the ocean and the cliffs."

"Would you show me some of your pictures?"

"Of course. I have some of the better ones on my laptop. I'll show you after dinner." Amelia wasn't above bribery to get the woman to eat. Loss of appetite was common in cancer patients, but it didn't stop Amelia from encouraging her. She'd gone as far as spending time in the kitchen with the cook, trying to come up with appetizing meals her patient might like better than others.

"I can't eat anymore. Can I see your pictures now?"

There would be no denying the older woman's plea. The eagerness in her faded eyes told Amelia of too few good moments in her life. Glancing over at the tray, Audrey had eaten at least half of her meal. She would take that as a win.

"Of course, let me clear these dishes away and I'll set it up."

Within minutes, the tray held Amelia's laptop, and she was showing Audrey how to flip through the photos with the mouse.

"I'm going to take the dishes to the kitchen while you go through the pictures. I won't be a minute."

"Take your time, child. I'll be fine," Audrey assured her, already clicking through the photos.

Maneuvering the tray through the doorway, she remembered the memory card still in her camera. She was grateful she hadn't uploaded it yet because that one held the pictures she'd snapped of Demetrius. She wasn't willing to answer the questions if they were discovered.

A shadow fell across her path as she pushed the cart past the stairway, and goosebumps rose on her arms. She didn't need to see him to know Geoffrey was there, waiting.

"You're a hard one to pin down."

Amelia took a deep breath. She couldn't afford to be rude to him, but it was taking everything she had just to speak to him.

"I told you before. I'm here to care for your great-grandmother, nothing more."

"Oh, I don't know about all that." A sly grin crossed his face, and he winked at her. "You found time for one admirer."

Amelia could feel the blood drain from her face. She remembered the upstairs curtain moving when she'd returned from the cliffs with Demetrius. Apparently, Geoffrey had been watching.

"What I do on my breaks is of no concern of yours."

Geoffrey stepped down from the stairs, crowding into her personal space. His hand covered hers on the tray handle, and Amelia was trapped in place. He was making this a habit.

"Does my mother know her hospice nurse is fooling around with a stranger on her breaks? She might not approve, you know."

Amelia yanked her hand out from under Geoffrey's and pushed the cart free.

"I'm not fooling around and I'm not neglecting Mrs. Marchand. You can quit stalking me. I'm sure you can find something else to do with your time."

Amelia fought the urge to run to the safety of the kitchen. She'd be damned if she gave Geoffrey the satisfaction of knowing how much he scared her. He did scare her though. Just the sight of him made her heart race, and not in a good way. There was something shifty about him, the way he seemed to see through her when he looked at her. Amelia felt like he was always planning something, and it couldn't be good, for anyone involved.

CHAPTER 10

The next morning Audrey was awake and waiting on Amelia.

"Did you have a bad night?" Amelia asked as she set up to take Audrey's vitals.

"No, I actually rested well, thank you. I have a lot on my mind, and I wanted to talk to you about it."

Amelia finished her routine before sitting down on the edge of the bed.

"What did you want to talk to me about?"

"Your pictures." Audrey's eyes were bright, and she was more alert than usual.

"You liked them?" Amelia took it as a good sign. Her patient needed something to take her mind away from her failing health.

Audrey struggled to sit up, then fell back helplessly against the pillow. "Help me sit up, child. I need to be able to think straight. Can't do that flat on my back."

With a chuckle, Amelia helped her to a comfortable sitting position. Tucking pillows around her, she stepped back.

"Better?"

Frail hands fluttered about her gown and the sheets before she settled. "This will do nicely. Now, come sit. We must discuss your future."

Her future. What in the world did Audrey have on her mind now?

"What do you mean, my future?"

"Your photography skills are excellent. You need to be selling those as prints. Julia can get in touch with one of her artsy friends. She knows several gallery owners. You'll have your own art showing. You'll make a name for yourself. Travel the world!"

Amelia couldn't help it, laughing at Audrey's exuberance.

"That's a pretty big dream."

"Dream nothing. I can make this happen. You're talented, girl. You can make money with your talent." A sudden coughing fit racked Audrey's frail body, and Amelia rushed to her side.

"You're getting too excited, Ms. Audrey. Calm down and drink a little water. I can't have you getting worse on my account." Audrey took small sips of water, then handed the glass back to Amelia.

"I'm fine, quit fussing." She grabbed Amelia's hand. "You're a good nurse, and a good person. I can help you if you let me."

Still holding Audrey's hand, Amelia sat beside her.

"It's not that I don't appreciate your offer, but I never thought about going further with my photography. I enjoy taking pictures and hope to take a course or two in the future to better my skills, but that's it."

"You should think about it. My offer still stands. I'll pay for your courses. Whatever you want. You have an eye for detail. Don't waste your talent."

"Thank you. I'll keep it in mind." Amelia smiled at her patient. "It's too chilly to go outside, but I can wheel you around the house if you'd like. Or would you like to watch some TV?"

"Hand me the phone, please. I need to make a few calls this morning. I want to take care of some business while I'm feeling better." She pulled the sheets tighter around her. "I'll need a pen and some paper too. I won't need you for the next hour."

Amused by the dismissal, Amelia made her way to the door.

"I'll be in my room if you need anything."

Audrey waved at her, already speaking to someone on the phone. Knowing she would be close and would hear Audrey if she called out, Amelia left.

Right before lunch, Amelia left her room only to find Julia coming out of Audrey's bedroom.

"Is everything all right? I told her I'd be in my room if she needed me," Amelia hurriedly explained.

"Everything is fine." Julia smiled warmly. "Grandmother is feeling quite spry today. She's 'in conference' with her attorney at the moment and doesn't wish to be disturbed. She has also asked for lunch to be served to them."

"Does she do this often?" Amelia asked, rubbing her chin.

"Not at all." Julia motioned for her to walk with her. "I don't think she's called Mr. Clayton in over a year. Her will was finalized some time ago and everything has been drawn up and readied at her request." She shook her head. "I have no idea what she's up to, and she's being close-mouthed about it."

"I hope she doesn't stress herself. She's going to have a setback if she overdoes it."

"Grandmother will be fine. She's stubborn as a mule when she sets her mind to something," Julia reassured her with a gentle pat on her arm. "I don't know if it would interest you but I'm going through some of Grandmother's papers and mementos. I was wondering if you would like to help me sort through them."

"If you think I would be able to help, I'm game." Amelia added, "When do you want to do it?"

"Well, it's not going to be done in one day." Julia laughed softly. "Grandmother was a bit of a packrat. There are several trunks in the attic. I figured I could tackle a little bit every day. I know Grandmother naps for a couple of hours after breakfast. Maybe then?" She added quickly, "I don't want to interfere with your afternoon break. You need to get out of the house when you can."

Amelia would never admit it aloud, but she was glad Julia added it in. She didn't want to give up her afternoon breaks or her precious time with Demetrius.

"Why don't we go up there now and see what we have on our hands?" Julia suggested. "Unless there was something else you were doing?"

"No, I was going to check on Ms. Audrey, but I'll wait until after lunch. I'm sure she will want to rest once her attorney leaves."

As they made their way up two flights of stairs, Amelia peeked down the halls. There was little to see with all the doors closed. Lovely vintage runner rugs lined the long hallways, and decorative tables held flower arrangements or framed pictures at each end. Sunlight coming through end windows lightened the otherwise darkened passages.

"These rooms have been closed off for years," Julia stopped short. "You know, I just realized you never got that tour of the house. What better time?" Striding down the hallway, Julia opened doors, then turned to find Amelia still standing in place near the stairs. She smiled brightly. "Come on, I think you'll like these."

Amelia ventured into each room as Julia told her a little about the room's artwork and furnishings. Each one was different, and they all had a name that stood out from the rest. The 'pink' room was aptly decorated in pinks and creams, the 'green' room had sage wallpaper, and so on. Julia made a game of it, making Amelia guess the room's names.

As they neared the end of rooms, Amelia found herself drawn to a window seat encased by bay windows. The view looked out over the ocean and she clearly saw the trail she took to get to the cliffs.

"Beautiful view, isn't it?"

Amelia turned to face Julia. "It is. I could spend hours sitting here."

As they left the room, there was only one unopened door remaining. Amelia looked curiously at Julia.

"That's Geoffrey's room," Julia informed her as they cleared the hall. She'd hesitated, as if mentioning her son was a subject she'd rather not get into.

Amelia felt goosebumps rise on her arms when she realized how clearly Geoffrey could see her returning from the cliffs from the view in his room. It was his curtains she'd seen that day. He'd been watching her from up here.

"Robert wants me to sell the house after Grandmother passes. It's been in the family for generations, but I feel my husband's right. This place is wasted on the two of us. We would be happier in a smaller home."

"What about your son? I gathered he was... attached to the place." Amelia was guessing, but he *had* called it his home the other night at the dinner table.

"Geoffrey never stays very long, he tends to come and go." Julia turned to face Amelia, her eyes large and bright with unshed tears. "Amelia, promise me you'll stay away from him. He's... troubled. I don't want you to get hurt."

Swallowing hard, she nodded. "Is there something specific I should know?" The woman's warning was ominous, but she was his mother, after all. This was becoming a difficult conversation.

Julia took a deep breath and shook her head. "I'm hoping it doesn't come to that."

Pulling a key from her pocket, Julia slipped it into the keyhole of a recessed door. She reached inside, and a row of bulbs cast dim circles of light, throwing eerie shadows in the corners. Amelia gasped as Julia opened the door wide. The attic was huge, filled with furniture, steamer trunks, and boxes. There must be generations of mementos stashed away. She had no idea how they were going to make sense of it all, much less find what Julia was looking for.

"A little daunting, isn't it?" Julia asked.

"Just a little," Amelia agreed. "Where do we start?"

"In that respect, we're in luck. Grandmother may have been a collector, but she was organized." She pointed to a corner on their left. "That section is hers, and those two trunks are what I need to go through. I need to see if there are any documents, policies, deeds... anything along that line."

Walking over to the trunks, Amelia pulled one away from the clutter.

"It doesn't sound too hard."

An hour later, Amelia was rethinking her initial impression. Julia had claimed the other steamer trunk, and they began with a vengeance. The more they discovered, the slower things went. There were so many loose pieces of paper. Amelia found bills of sale dating back over fifty years, letters to and from people in Audrey's past, and dozens of old photos.

Coming across a photo of a much younger Julia and Robert, Amelia glanced over at Julia, dusty and grimy as she peered over a stack of papers.

"How did you and Robert meet?"

Julia looked up, spotting the curled photo in Amelia's hand. Taking it from her she studied it, a smile slowly spreading across her face.

"This was taken our first Christmas together," Julia reminisced. "I was one of the few Marchand women who decided to venture out and get a job." She rolled her eyes. "There was no need for it, financially, we were quite well off, but I didn't want to sit home either. So, I went to college, got my Bachelor's, then my Master's. I landed a job at a bank in Portland, Maine shortly after.

That's where I met Robert. He was a financial consultant at the bank and we literally met over the water cooler." Julia laughed over the memory. "He was so witty and charming. I think I fell for him immediately." She glanced at the photo once again. "We dated for several months before I finally brought him home to meet the family. I was so nervous. But it was for nothing, Robert won them over as easily as he did me. We married a year later, and here we are."

Amelia would've asked more questions, but that would have led to talk of children and the last thing she wanted to hear was anything to do with Geoffrey. Turning her attention back to the trunk in front of her, she pulled out another stack of papers.

Picking out a yellowed folded piece of paper, Amelia opened it—a sketch of Demetrius stared back at her. The likeness was uncanny, but there was no mistaking him for anyone else. There was a faint print on the bottom corner of the page. Amelia pushed her glasses up, squinting at the scrawl—*Alexander Demetrius Matteo*. Staring at the picture in shock, Amelia couldn't get her brain to function. It couldn't be. There was no way. *This* was Audrey's love, Alexander? She knew about strong genetics, but this... this was too much!

"Is something wrong, Amelia?"

"No." Amelia cleared her throat. "I, uh, it must be the dust." She pointed at a stack of papers beside her.

"I'll run down and get us a couple of bottles of water." Julia rose from her own stack. "This is turning into dirty work." She glanced back at Amelia before she cleared the door. "You look like you saw a ghost. Why don't you take a break until I come back up with the water?"

"Sure, okay." Swallowing hard, Amelia stared down at the sketch again. A ghost, indeed. Was this Demetrius' grandfather? Or... no, it couldn't be. A vampire? Could this be Demetrius? She was so confused. It had to be a family resemblance. That was it. But then again, she remembered Demetrius telling her he knew Audrey—from a long time ago. She rubbed her arms, a sudden chill running through her veins.

Carefully folding the sketch, she slipped it into her pocket. She would get to the bottom of this one way or the other. But who would she confront, Audrey or Demetrius?

CHAPTER 11

Checking on Audrey after lunch, she found her patient nodding off, propped up on too many pillows, and hurried to her side.

"Let's get you more comfortable. Would you like something for pain so you can rest better?" she coaxed.

"Thank you, dear." Audrey nodded sleepily. "I'm afraid I wore myself out this morning,"

"I was afraid of that. No matter, we'll get you situated, then you can sleep."

Giving the woman her pain pills, she swallowed them with no trouble. A few minutes more, and Audrey was comfortable. A murmured "thank you" and she was drifting off before Amelia had finished tidying up the room.

As Audrey slept, Amelia took her chance. She was going to call Demetrius to see if he could meet her on the cliffs. The drawing pulled at her. She needed to know the truth of the matter. Her only nagging doubt was, could she trust him?

By the time Audrey was sleeping soundly, and Amelia was dressed for outdoors, it was nearing mid-afternoon. Peering out the window, the day was overcast but not threatening rain like the last time. There were occasional wind gusts, but it was the norm for this time of year.

Picking up her cell phone, she punched in Demetrius' number. After four rings, she was about to end the call when he answered.

"Matteo."

"Demetrius? It's Amelia."

His voice went from businesslike to sensual in an instant, his reply caressing her like a warm embrace.

"Amelia! I didn't know if you would call. I'm glad you did."

The timbre of his voice resonated deep within her. It took all her willpower to focus on the reason for the call, and not get sidetracked.

"I was going up to the cliffs, and I wondered if you would meet me. I need to speak to you."

"Of course. I can leave now if you'd like."

"Thank you. I'll see you in a few minutes."

Ending the call, she bit her bottom lip in consternation. Slipping her phone into her pocket, her fingers touched the stiff, folded paper. She had no idea how this conversation was going to go. With Audrey's talk of vampires and a sketch more than fifty years old, it was going to be hard to believe either way.

Slipping out the back door, Amelia was grateful she didn't run into Geoffrey. For all she knew, he was watching her leave from an upstairs window, but it couldn't be helped. Geoffrey and his troubles would have to wait. She had more pressing matters. As she reached the trail, a blast of cold air hit her. Pulling her hood up, she picked up her pace. She figured Demetrius would get there about the same time.

If she continued to see him, they might need to relocate their trysts. The open cliffs were going to be brutal as winter moved in, but Amelia wasn't sure she would even be here through the winter. Audrey was doing well today, but she wasn't going to get any better. Truth be known, Amelia didn't expect the elderly woman to last much longer. It was going to be a hard Christmas for Julia.

Amelia didn't see Demetrius immediately. He was standing still as a statue, leaning against the gates to the small cemetery, his expression guarded.

Reaching for her, he kissed her lightly on the lips. A strong hand caressed her cheek as he studied her.

"Something is bothering you. What has happened?"

She shook her head, trying to gather her thoughts.

"What makes you say that?"

"You pulled away from my kiss. Why, Amelia?"

Stunned, she had no answer, wasn't even aware she'd done it. Heat scorched her cheeks. Fumbling in her pocket, she pulled out the drawing.

"Julia and I were going through some of Ms. Audrey's papers, and I found this." She handed him the sketch.

Demetrius took it from her, his gaze never leaving her face. As he opened it, he glanced down, studied it briefly, then stared out at the waves as he folded it, handing it back to her.

"What has Audrey told you?"

Amelia's throat constricted; her breathing labored. This was not the response she expected nor wanted. What was he implying? Was Audrey's tale of a vampire true? How could this be? She couldn't walk away without knowing the truth. Even if the truth was so unbelievable—she had to know. Forcing herself to meet his gaze, Amelia told him.

"Audrey told me about her first love, a young man named Alexander. She also told me he was a vampire. He left her because he didn't want to make her like him. He wanted her to have a normal life. She always loved him, but after several years, she married and had a family. She's never forgotten him." She held up the folded paper. "Then I found this. It's an incredible likeness, and it bears your name." She took a deep breath. "What am I supposed to think, Demetrius? Or is it Alexander?"

"She always had a talent for sketching." He ran a hand through his thick unruly hair. "I was unaware she'd drawn that."

Amelia stared at him. "Would you have destroyed it if you'd known?"

"Perhaps."

"So, it's true."

He reached for her but pulled back before she could refuse him.

"Amelia, will you hear me out?"

It was Amelia's turn to stare out at the churning water far below. A part of her found it strange she wasn't afraid of him. She'd come to care for this mysterious man. In spite of the unbelievable unfolding before her, Amelia wanted to hear what he had to say, wanted to understand—wanted to know the truth. With tears in her eyes, she nodded mutely.

"Come."

She stepped back. "Where are we going?"

"Amelia, please." He ran his hand through his hair again.

Amelia's fingers itched to run through his wild, unruly hair, but she clamped down on those urges. *He's a vampire for crying out loud and you want to jump his bones?*

"I want to take you to my house. We can talk in comfort. I swear you are safe with me. I would never harm you."

She was torn. Amelia wanted to go with him. Before she found the sketch, she would have been overjoyed at the invitation. Now, she didn't know what to do. Looking into those dark, liquid eyes, the depth of his feelings was obvious. She'd trusted him up to this point. She would take a leap of faith.

Extending her hand, he took it, twining their fingers together, and softly kissed her fingertips.

"I promise no harm will come to you."

The walk to his home was made in silence. Amelia didn't know what to say or ask, figuring it would be better to listen and hear Demetrius out. She had no idea what was going to happen from this point on. Apparently, Alex and Demetrius were the same person. Would he leave her as he'd left Audrey all those years ago? A lump lodged in her throat and tears threatened behind shuttered lids. She cared so much in the little time she'd known him. Losing him would leave a gaping hole in her heart. And she hadn't yet heard his side of the story.

Demetrius led her up the walk to a modest home, compared to all the mansions she'd seen so far. Towering pines surrounded the two-story retreat, an enclosed verandah and a stone chimney giving it a cozy charm Amelia found appealing.

He opened the door, motioning for her to step through. Amelia hesitated only a moment before entering. Warmth surrounding her, she unzipped her jacket, which was suddenly heavy and constricting.

Demetrius slipped it from her shoulders, murmuring, "Your jacket will be right here on the coat rack when you are ready to leave."

Amelia couldn't fault him. He was giving her the option to leave when she chose, making it clear she wasn't a prisoner. She was here of her own volition.

"Please, have a seat." He walked to the fireplace, adding another log to the small, flickering flames. "Would you care for something to drink?"

She shook her head. "No, thank you. I'm fine."

Pointing to the space beside her, Demetrius asked, "May I?"

Pushing her glasses up, she nodded.

He reached for her hands, his thumbs rubbing small circles over the tops of hers.

"I guess I should start at the beginning. Though I'm not sure which beginning to start with... mine or when I met Audrey."

"Tell me about you first. Is your name Alexander or Demetrius?"

"Both, actually." He laughed, the sound low and deep. "Alexander Demetrius Matteo is my full name. For now, I go by Demetrius. I change names every generation or so to avoid questions. For the same reason, I tend to move often."

"How long have you been like..."—she waved her fingers— "this?"

His gaze penetrated her own, the angles of his face in sharp relief from the light of the fireplace behind them.

"I have been a vampire for over a thousand years. I am one of the Ancients. There are only a few of us left."

Amelia's mind raced. She never believed in vampires, yet here she was, sitting in front of one claiming to be over a thousand years old!

"I don't know what to say or ask. I never accepted the belief of the supernatural. I always thought it was made-up fairy tales."

"How do you think those fairy tales started?" Demetrius chuckled. "There's usually a grain of truth in all stories."

His expression turned somber. "Though my beginnings were hardly a fairy tale. I was raised by my mother, who was a seamstress. We were poor but my mother took care of me the best she could. I never knew my father."

"When I was old enough, I joined the military. Through hard work, perseverance, and sheer luck I advanced, becoming a junior officer under the Byzantine general, Constantine Arianites. During battle, we suffered a heavy defeat, and I was mortally injured on the field. I woke days later in a cave with an unquenchable thirst for blood. I had no idea what I had become or who made me that way. It took me a long time to figure out what had happened and how I was to survive."

"How did you figure it all out?"

"Mostly trial and error." His laugh was bitter. "If I ventured out into the sun, I'd burn. It didn't take me long to figure out I could only travel by night. After that, I spent my time searching for answers. A crone in a nearby village provided information in the form of ancient lore, giving me enough to survive on. It was years before I could control my urges."

She tried desperately to come up with some sort of intelligent question to ask, finally blurting out, "But I've seen you in the daylight. Aren't all vampires creatures of the night?" She blushed furiously, having referred to him as a creature, though he didn't take offense at her blunder.

"As a rule, yes." Unbuttoning his shirt, he pulled aside the material to expose a tattoo on his left pec. "This is the *Vergina Sun*. I hired a Macedonian mage eight hundred years ago to do the work. It's imbued with magic, allowing me to walk in the sun. While I am immortal, I can still be killed, though sunlight will never be one of the ways."

"But you drink blood to survive?"

"Yes," Demetrius sighed heavily, "that part is true. However, I think of myself as civilized and have arrangements for bagged blood to be delivered wherever I reside. Because of my age, I don't require constant feeding. I can go days without sustenance."

"Do you ever feed from a person?" she asked, unable to meet his eyes.

He reached over and lifted her chin, making her meet his gaze.

"I will never lie to you, my Amelia. If the party is willing, yes. But the days of taking an unwilling donor are long behind me."

She had to take him at his word. There was no other way to know if he was telling the truth.

"Tell me about Audrey."

Demetrius traced an elegant finger along his brow, taking his time before he answered.

"Audrey Marchand was beautiful, charming, and intelligent. She was a ray of sunshine among all the other girls in her social circle. I was drawn to her, I will not deny it. I even loved her, in my fashion, but it was in vain and could not last. At her father's urging, she pressed to know why I wouldn't attend any of her day functions."

Amelia gave him a sharp glance. "You said you could walk in the sun. Why didn't you go with her?"

Demetrius met her gaze, dark brown eyes pleading with her to understand.

"It was one thing to spend time with her in the evenings when we were relatively alone, but her day functions were another thing entirely, filled with groups of people and other couples. It would have been taken for granted we were bound for marriage. I couldn't let that happen."

"But you said you loved her!" Amelia struggled to understand.

"I did... in my own fashion." He pulled her closer, his larger hands engulfing hers against his hard chest. "I am so very old, Amelia. I have known countless women, had untold affairs. I'm no saint, but there has never been a woman I wanted to spend eternity with, and that includes Audrey." He released her hands, fingering one of her long curls. "I was doomed to be alone... until I met you."

Amelia tensed, her gaze locking with his. "What are you saying?"

"I love you, Amelia." His words were soft as a whisper on the breeze. "You have captured my heart. If I had a soul, it would be yours. I want nothing more than to spend the rest of my days with you."

She couldn't think, couldn't breathe. One part of her thrilled at his words, another chastised herself for being ridiculous.

"But I'll grow old, like Audrey. And you... you'll always be young."

Demetrius's dark eyes softened. "It doesn't have to be like that."

CHAPTER 12

Amelia sat patiently in the passenger seat of the Audi as Demetrius went around to let her out. They'd hardly said a word on the short drive to the cottage. She had a lot to think about, and it wasn't something she was going to decide overnight. Taking her hand, he helped her from the car, leaning in to kiss her softly on the lips.

"Think about it, Amelia. I'm not pushing for an answer. I know it's a lot to process. All I ask for is a chance. Call me if you want to talk. Call me if you need me." The look of anguish on his face was almost too much for her to bear. "Promise me you'll call."

"I will, I promise. Just give me time to think."

Leaving her on the steps, he drove away. When she'd left the house earlier, it was in search of answers. Now, she was afraid she'd gotten more than she'd bargained for.

Realizing she didn't have a key to the front door, Amelia slipped around to the back. She couldn't help but wonder what Geoffrey would think when she didn't come up the trail as usual. If she stayed close to the house, he wouldn't see her slip in the back door.

Closing the door behind her, a small thrill of triumph went through her that no one was around to witness her arrival. Padding to her room, she changed her clothes and hurried to check on her patient. Glancing at her watch, she'd been away an hour longer than usual. She hoped Ms. Audrey hadn't been waiting on her. Amelia was so mentally drained, she wouldn't be able to come up with a creative excuse for her absence.

Entering the elderly woman's room, she breathed a sigh of relief. Audrey was sleeping soundly, soft snores coming from the bed. Amelia sat in her usual corner chair and pulled out her laptop. She could upload the last of her pictures while she waited on her patient to wake.

Her finger stilled on the tiny mouse when she came to the shots of Demetrius. Apparently, the myth of vampires not having a reflection was just that. He stood in the middle of her frame, solid flesh and bone. Demetrius was a beautiful man—dark, brooding, angles and hard planes. Her breath caught as she stared at his picture. There was no doubt she was in love with him— she just didn't know if she could be with him.

Saving his picture to a secured folder, she closed the laptop. At this point, she didn't want anyone to see the pictures of Demetrius. She had the sketch tucked away in her suitcase. She would protect his secret.

Movement from the bed caught her attention and Amelia rose to check on her patient. Audrey's eyes fluttered open, blinking to focus on her.

Amelia smiled brightly. "Hello there, Ms. Audrey. Did you rest well?"

"Not really, dear. I'm so tired." Blue-veined hands trembled as they attempted to pull the covers up. "What time is it?"

"It's close to six, you've been sleeping all afternoon." Amelia straightened the sheets around her until she was comfortable again. "Would you like something to eat?"

"I'm not hungry." Audrey waved her away. "I'm going to sleep some more. Why don't you have dinner with Julia and Robert? I'm sure they would enjoy your company."

Audrey drifted back off to sleep. Amelia finished tucking her in and recorded her vitals before turning out the light and slipping from the room. She would check on her before she turned in for the night. Right now, sleep was the best medicine for her patient.

The look of delight on Julia and Robert's faces as she walked into the dining room made Amelia ashamed. These people had been nothing but kind to her, and she'd hidden away in her patient's room because of Geoffrey. She was an adult, the least she could do was act like one. She could handle herself in uncomfortable situations... at least she hoped she could. So far, she hadn't been doing all that well.

"Amelia! I'm so glad you decided to join us," Julia exclaimed. "Is Grandmother still sleeping? I checked on her once while you were out. She was sleeping so soundly I didn't dare stay in her room for fear of waking her."

"She woke long enough to tell me she wasn't hungry and was going back to sleep." She smiled at the couple as she eased into her chair. "I'm afraid her little meeting this morning wore her out. She's not as strong as she thinks she is."

"You're right, Amelia." Robert nodded in agreement. "In her day, she was a force to be reckoned with. Now, she's a pale shadow of herself."

Julia's face fell at her husband's words.

"It's the truth. Grandmother kept this family going for so long. When my parents were killed in an auto crash several years ago, it took a toll on her. She's outlived practically everyone, family, and friends. Now, she's dealing with cancer, and there's little fight left in her."

"She's lived a long, full life. Listening to her talk about her youth, I think she's at peace and has accepted her end. I'm going to help her through the transition as much as possible. I've grown to love her, and don't want to see her suffer more than necessary."

Julia wiped a tear from her cheek. "You've been a blessing to us, Amelia. I'm so grateful the agency sent you."

"How touching!" Geoffrey's harsh voice grated across the room. Pulling back a chair, he joined them at the table. "Has our little angel of mercy won your heart, Mother?"

Amelia blanched. Unused to Geoffrey's brand of crudeness, she wanted to flee from the room, only her determination to stick it out keeping her in her seat.

Robert slammed his hand on the table. "That's enough, Geoffrey!"

The belligerent sneer on Geoffrey's face showed a violent side that scared Amelia. She had no doubt, the man was dangerous. How was she going to manage to stay long enough to care for Audrey and stay off Geoffrey's radar?

"What are you going to do, Robert? Send me back?"

Robert's face flushed with anger. "If you keep up this type of behavior, you can count on it."

Geoffrey leaned over the table, a steak knife gripped tightly in one hand.

"I don't think you want to make that mistake." Flinging the knife across the table, he stormed out of the room.

Robert, still as a statue, took a deep breath, then addressed his wife.

"Tell her, Julia."

Julia sent a panicked look toward Amelia.

"Tell her *now*, she deserves to know."

Julia swallowed hard, her hand shaking as she attempted to drink from a heavy crystal goblet. Water splashed onto the table and she set the glass down.

"You're right." She met Amelia's gaze. "I'm so sorry, I should have told you when he first arrived. Robert is not Geoffrey's father. He's my son from a previous marriage. My son has been in and out of mental institutions for the past ten years." Her voice dropped to a whisper as tears streamed down her cheeks. "He's diagnosed as a psychopath. He's extremely violent, Amelia."

Julia took a deep breath before continuing. "Geoffrey was always a difficult child, always a bit different from the other children. When I caught him torturing small animals, I knew I had a problem. He's been in therapy since he was eleven." She nervously twisted a lock of brown hair. "Geoffrey has been through several psychiatrists; none have seemed to be able to help. It all came to a head when he was seventeen. A young girl from town came up missing. When her body was finally found..." Julia shuddered at the memory. "Her body was found in the woods near the cliffs. She'd been tortured. Geoffrey's fingerprints were found on a knife with her blood on it. He was arrested, but my family money kept him from prison. Instead, he's spent the last several years in a mental institution."

Robert reached over, squeezing Julia's hand, then faced Amelia.

"To be honest, we don't understand why he was released. According to his doctor, Geoffrey is capable of rehabilitative treatment. Obviously, the doctor is mistaken." He gave his wife a worried look, then continued, "All of Julia's family money has been spent on Geoffrey's medical care. There's nothing left to send him back to a private hospital. We have spent all our time and Julia's money on protecting him from the criminal courts and prisons. He's on his own now."

"What would you have me do?" Amelia's thoughts were jumbled. She had an obligation to fulfill her duty to Audrey but was terrified for her safety with a psychopath in the house. For that matter, Julia and

Robert were scared for their own safety. What could be done about any of it?

Julia fought to compose herself. Blotting away the tears, she sat straighter. Giving her husband a tremulous smile, she then faced Amelia.

"If you would be agreeable, I would like you to stay with Grandmother—in her room, with the door locked. I will personally bring your trays to you. I will not allow him to hurt you, Amelia."

Amelia sat quietly, thinking. Audrey didn't have much longer. She'd given up and was waiting to pass. Amelia had seen it often enough to know the signs, but she hadn't said anything to Julia or Robert. Another day or two, and she would be free to leave. Surely, she could deal with everything else for that long.

"I'll stay, and I'll keep to our rooms, with the doors locked. You have the keys?"

Julia nodded and stood. "I'll get them for you."

As she left the room, Robert gave her a warm smile.

"Thank you, Amelia. I know this is a lot to ask, and I'm grateful for your decision. Julia is trying to be strong, but she has so much on her shoulders right now. Geoffrey is impossible to deal with."

"I can't even imagine how she does it. Or you either, for that matter."

Julia entered, bearing two skeleton keys in her hand. Giving them to Amelia, she instructed, "The one with the white tape is Grandmother's, the one with the blue is yours. There are no other keys like those, so you don't have to worry about copies floating about."

"Thanks." Amelia took the keys, pocketing them. "I'm going to grab a few things from my room and

102

spend the night with Ms. Audrey. I'll see you in the morning."

Demetrius knelt before the fireplace, reflexively poking at the logs, oblivious to the sparks flying from the rapidly growing flames. Deep in thought, he wondered about his long life, how one path often aligned with another. He'd given in to the urge, almost a compulsion, to return to Boothbay Harbor. Demetrius hadn't been back since he'd left Audrey all those many years ago. But now he was back. Had it been to say goodbye to an old love or was it to meet a new one?

One thing was certain, his focus was single minded, everything centered on—Amelia. He'd told her the truth about himself, all of it. He'd no regrets in telling her, but was fearful of her decision regarding him, and them together. Amelia was different. He wanted her to come to him willingly, under her own volition.

She loved him, he knew that. But was it enough? Amelia was young and innocent, a mere child to his many, many years. What would she know of everlasting love and enduring trials of time? Would she be willing to give him the chance to show her what a life with him could hold?

He let out a heavy sigh as he replaced the poker on the rack of irons. Easing into a chair, he stared moodily at the flames. Demetrius couldn't remember the last time he'd felt the flare of emotion that tore through him now. In all his long years, he'd never felt the strong emotion toward another as he did for Amelia.

He thought back to another Ancient, the one known simply as Xavier. The Immortal had been alone for millennia before he met Contessa. They'd been together for over a thousand years now and were still a vital force. Demetrius realized he wanted what they had.

For the first time in his long life, he wanted a woman by his side. Not just any woman, but Amelia. What he felt for her was so much more than what he'd felt for Audrey, or countless others before. Why now? Why Amelia? What was it about her that called to him?

Those were questions he couldn't answer. But he'd learned one thing in all his years. He was a patient man. He had time to figure it out.

CHAPTER 13

Amelia was headed to her room when Audrey called out. Her things could wait, she needed to tend to her patient. She entered the room, locking the door behind her, pocketing the keys. Finding Ms. Audrey awake, she walked to the bedside and sat down beside her.

"Is there anything I can do for you, Ms. Audrey? Are you hungry? I can get you something to eat, if you'd like."

The woman waved away Amelia's offers.

"I need to tell you something. Come sit beside me, child." Once Amelia was settled, Audrey continued, her voice papery thin. "I don't have much longer." Despite her failing health and weakened state, her grip was fierce on Amelia's arm. "Don't interrupt. You need to listen to me. My time has come. After I pass, I want you to get out of here. Pack your things and leave. It's for your own safety. My lawyers will see to your pay and a bonus for being a friend as well as my nurse."

The effort of talking sent her into a coughing fit. Amelia helped her to sit up, cushioning her against a stack of pillows. After helping her sip some water, she nodded she was able to go on.

"Thank you, Amelia. Now, promise me, you'll do as I say. I don't want you in this house a moment longer with Geoffrey. The boy is pure evil. He may be half my blood, but the other half is Satan's spawn. Lord knows poor Julia has suffered enough because of him. She doesn't realize I know what happened to all my money."

"The pain is worse." The woman laid back against the pillows, clearly exhausted. "Could you get something to help ease me along?" Her eyes pleaded for relief from suffering.

"Of course, I'll get what you need right now." Amelia nodded as she situated Audrey into a comfortable position.

Going to the mini-fridge tucked inside the closet, Amelia prepared what would probably be the last morphine cocktail for her patient. She was reasonably sure Audrey wouldn't see the morning.

Once Audrey drifted off, she headed to her own room to gather a few things. Her attention was drawn to a lilac-colored box on her bed. The label attached to the ribbon was from the shop where she'd bought her dress. Opening the box, she pushed aside the silver tissue paper to find an ivory satin gown with a matching robe. The fabric slipped through her fingers. She'd never owned anything so beautiful. Dropping the gown to the bed, she rummaged through the box and tissue paper looking for a card, hoping to find who'd given her such a luxurious gift. Her search came up with nothing. Had Demetrius sent it to the house? Why didn't Rachel let her know about the package instead of just leaving it on the bed?

Picking up the gown and wrapper, she draped them over her arm as she gathered what she would need for the night. Next time she saw Demetrius, she would thank him for the beautiful gift. Tonight, she would wear it and think of him.

Emerging from the en suite, Amelia gently ran her hands over the satin gown. Just touching the smooth material made her feel pretty. This probably wasn't the appropriate time or place to wear something so exquisite, but she liked the way it made her feel.

Settling into her corner of the room, Amelia emailed her parents. She'd already informed them of her plans to travel, both as an agency nurse and for pleasure. It would be awhile before she returned to her hometown, but she would keep the apartment until she decided what she was going to do with her future.

Which of course led to Demetrius. Who would ever believe she'd fallen in love with a vampire? She would have never entertained such a thing even existed—before Demetrius—but there he was, solid and very real. Leaving and never seeing him again left an emptiness in her heart. She wanted him in her life, but could she enter a relationship with a vampire?

She remembered when she'd protested about growing old and he wouldn't. He'd told her it didn't have to be like that. Was he willing to change her to become like him? Was that what she wanted? She didn't have the answers, didn't know if she would ever have them.

A tap at the door drew her from her deep thoughts. Unlocking and cracking the door open slightly, she was relieved to see it was only Julia.

"I wanted to make sure you were all right. I feel so horrible about everything tonight." She twisted her hands helplessly. "I should have been honest with you from the beginning about my son. You should have been given the option to leave."

Her anguish tore at Amelia. Closing the door behind her, she attempted to calm the older woman.

"I seriously doubt I would have left, regardless. Your grandmother needs me, that's the important thing." She met Julia's gaze. "You need to know something too." She took a deep breath, then continued. "Ms. Audrey probably won't last the night. She's ready to go. Patients usually know when it's their time. Would you like to sit with her for a little bit? She's sleeping, but it would probably be your last chance to say goodbye."

Julia's eyes filled with tears. "Thank you, Amelia. I'd like that."

Quietly, they entered the room. Amelia went back to her corner chair, and Julia eased onto the side of the bed. She gently held her grandmother's hand, sitting in silence. After a few minutes, Julia said in a whisper, "Amelia?"

"Yes?" Amelia put down the book she'd been staring at.

"I... I think she's gone."

Crossing the room to get her stethoscope, she traded places with Julia. She was right. Audrey Marchand had simply stopped breathing, passing in her sleep peacefully. She marked the time and called the coroner's office from the list of emergency numbers taped to the older woman's bedside table. Removing the I.V. from her patient's arm, Amelia automatically went through the post-mortem care, preparing for the coroner's arrival.

"What do we do now?" Julia asked.

"I called the coroner. He'll come and pronounce her deceased, then take her body to the funeral home. You've already made arrangements, right?"

"I did." Julia nodded as she wiped away a trail of tears. "Everything is in place. I need to tell Robert." She tried to smile, but it fell short. "I need a drink. How about you, Amelia? A shot of whiskey to get us through this?"

"I'm not much for whiskey, but I'll get you a glass. I'll meet you back here."

Padding barefoot to the living room, Amelia eased behind the bar. As she reached for a glass, a voice from the darkness startled her.

"So, our little nurse isn't quite so saintly, after all. Having a drink on the job?"

Amelia bit back a curse as the tumbler rolled across the bar. Grabbing for it, she shot back, "Is it really any of your business what I do?" She didn't feel the need to expound on her actions.

Geoffrey stepped out of the shadows, eyeing her up and down.

"Aren't you a delectable vision? That's a far cry from the scrubs you wear every day."

"Is there something you want, Geoffrey?" Amelia's patience was thin enough around him. Compounded with Audrey's death, she'd rather do without his presence if possible.

"Well, if you're going to wear my gift, you should at least have a drink with me."

"What? *Your* gift?" Amelia froze in place, a sinking feeling in the pit of her stomach. "You gave me this gown?"

"Who else? Surely not your friend from the cliffs. He would never have got the package into the house." He eased toward Amelia.

"I've been watching you for quite a while. In fact, I was watching you before I 'officially' returned."

Amelia's heart raced, fear pumping through her veins. She'd been right. Someone *had* been watching her all this time and it had been Geoffrey.

"Don't think I don't know what Mother and Robert told you about me." He gave her a sly smile. "They wonder how I was released from the institution considering my violent nature. It took some time and planning but I finally set up a golden opportunity. I forced that doctor to sign my release and then he 'conveniently' had a heart attack," Geoffrey feigned a look of innocence, but his eyes belied his true nature. "It's amazing how some people react to stark fear. Paperwork was shuffled in with his other work, his office was empty when he was found—" Geoffrey inched closer to her. "Did I mention there was no record of an appointment with me that day? No one knew I'd been there."

Boxed in a corner, Amelia had nowhere to go. Her heart pounded as she furiously tried to figure out the best way out of this dilemma. One thing for sure, she couldn't let Geoffrey get to her. There was no doubt in her mind he was violent and dangerous—he was, after all, diagnosed as a psychopath. *Didn't he just confess to causing the death of his doctor?* There weren't any nice guys in those padded rooms. She didn't want to scream, alerting Julia and Robert. There was no telling what Geoffrey would do if he felt threatened by all of them in the same room.

Geoffrey grabbed her arm, pushing her against the wall and trailed a finger along her jawline.

"Pretty little Amelia, the gown looks good on you, but I bet it would look even better on the floor around your dainty little feet."

Amelia swallowed hard. She couldn't let him do this! Pushing him as hard as she could, she unbalanced him enough to release her. Sweeping her arm across the bar, she latched onto a wooden handle. On pure adrenaline and reflex, she stabbed him in the stomach. The corkscrew buried deep in his soft flesh and Geoffrey yelled in pain.

Amelia tore away from the bar, managing to evade his grasp. Sprinting for the front door, Amelia was out and running before Geoffrey could catch her.

Heart pounding and gasping for air, Amelia ran for her life—straight toward the woods. The wind whipped her long, thick hair into her face, blinding her as she fought desperately to get away from the manor house.

Rocks tore at her bare feet as she struggled to keep her balance on the uneven ground. Her thin gown and wrapper were useless against the chill in the air.

Thunder reverberated in the sky as lightning strikes filled the air with an eerie light. As the storm gained momentum, so did the waves crashing against the cliffs. Huge drops of cold rain pelted Amelia as she slipped and stumbled toward the safety of the trees.

She'd been told not to venture into the forest, that there were bears, wolves, and other creatures. At this point, she'd gladly seek sanctuary with wild animals before she'd go back to that house—to the threat waiting inside.

Amelia peered over her shoulder, fearful she was being followed. Someone called her name, but it could have been the wind howling and whipping through the trees. She screamed when a limb caught at her hair, a burning sting across her cheek when she yanked the small branch out, losing long strands of hair by the roots. In the struggle to free herself, Amelia wasn't paying attention to the path. The rain had quickly turned the dirt to mud, and she lost her footing. Falling hard, she fought not to scream again as she scrambled to her feet. Gulping air into her burning lungs, thankful she wasn't injured, she dashed up the path.

For the first time in longer than she could remember, Amelia prayed. All she wanted was to get out of this nightmare. She needed to get to the cliffs. If she could get there, she'd be safe.

Wet, muddy satin bunched in her hands, Amelia made her way toward the cemetery. She grabbed at the slippery material before she tripped again. Strong arms caught her, and she screamed.

Demetrius dropped the wine glass on the tile floor, shards of glass splintering in all directions, dark red wine staining the light colored tiles. He clutched at his head, pain gripping in an unrelenting vise. Amelia. She was in danger. He needed to go to her now!

Without thought to the elements, he raced through the night with inhuman speed. He needed to get to the cliffs. She would be there.

He found Amelia stumbling toward the cemetery. Catching her before she fell, she cried out.

"Deme... Demetrius? Is it really you?"

"Yes, *mikros*, it's me. I felt your fear. Tell me what has sent you out in this storm in your nightclothes."

He held her close, her heart pounding like the thrumming of a hummingbird's wings.

"Ms. Audrey passed away tonight. Julia went to tell her husband and asked me to get her a drink. While I was getting it, Geoffrey cornered me."

At the mention of his name, Demetrius hissed, his vision grew hazy, clouded with crimson, then sharpened. Amelia pulled from his embrace.

"Demetrius?"

"It's all right, Amelia," pulling her back into his arms. "You're safe with me. I'll protect you."

"There you are, you little slut!"

A man staggered toward them, clutching his stomach. Blood poured from a ragged wound and Demetrius' fangs punched through his gums. The metallic scent was strong and enticing despite the wind whipping around them.

Demetrius stepped in front of Amelia, blocking her from viewing the man's approach.

"You'll never lay another hand on Amelia, I can promise you," Demetrius snarled.

"Figures the bitch would run straight to you," Geoffrey grunted. "It doesn't matter, you'll both go down." Pulling a gun from his jacket, he leveled it at Demetrius and fired.

The wind howled, but the gunshot blasted over the storm. Amelia screamed when the impact of the shot pushed him against her. There was no time to explain to her that bullets couldn't harm him. He turned to her, shoving her toward the cemetery.

"Get behind a crypt and stay there," he ordered.

Thankfully, she'd listened to him. Out of the corner of his eye he saw her fumble with the iron gate until she managed to open it, slipping inside. She staggered over to the largest crypt, ducking behind it.

Demetrius strode toward the man who would dare to attack Amelia. With one hand, he picked Geoffrey up by the throat, lifting him above the ground, feet dangling helplessly. With his other hand, he yanked the gun free from his grasp, tossing it over the edge of the cliff.

"You cannot harm me, and you will never harm Amelia or anyone else!"

Demetrius' fangs grew in length. Geoffrey screamed in horror as the truth revealed what Demetrius truly was, but it was too late. With a jerk, Demetrius pulled Geoffrey to him, ripping out his throat. The taste of his blood was rich and heady, but he forced himself to stop. He would not drain this scum in front of Amelia. Walking to the edge of the cliffs, he threw the body over the edge.

Demetrius lifted his face to the pouring rain, letting nature wash away the gruesome evidence of Geoffrey's death.

Amelia stepped out from the crypt, cautiously making her way to him. The cold rain sluiced down their bodies as she stood in front of him.

"You now know exactly what kind of monster I am. I will see you back to the manor house and will not bother you again."

"No! You promised you would stay with me!"

Perplexed, he faced her, reaching for her hands.

"You still want me?" He motioned toward the cliffs. "After what I just did?"

Tears streamed down her cheeks as she shivered from the cold.

"I love you, Demetrius. I accept what you are. I don't want you to leave."

Stunned by her words, he scooped her into his arms, cradling her against his hard chest. He kissed her softly, grateful for her love. Lightning streaked across the sky and the wind howled as the rain picked up once more. Amelia needed shelter and warmth. He would care for her needs, now and always.

CHAPTER 14

"Are you sure this is what you want, *agápi mou*?"

Amelia nodded against his chest. "It's better this way. As soon as I get all this," —she motioned to the flashing lights outside the cottage— "straightened out, I'll be free to leave. I'll call you as soon as I can."

Demetrius gently lowered Amelia to the ground.

"I don't like you going in there alone."

"If you come with me, there will be even more questions." Her thoughts went back to Geoffrey. "I'm sticking with my story. Geoffrey attacked me, I defended myself, and ran out of the house. He followed me up to the cliffs. He grabbed for me but tripped and fell over the edge to the rocks below."

Demetrius whispered in her ear, "And then wolves found the body and ripped out his throat?"

Fear clutched her, and she raised panicked eyes to Demetrius.

"Don't worry. I'll take care of Geoffrey. It will indeed appear to be an animal attack."

She gave him a worried look, but he turned her around, gently shoving her toward the cottage.

"Go. You have enough to deal with."

Amelia straightened her shoulders and walked to the house. She was wet and sure she looked like something the cat dragged in, but she would look everyone square in the eye. She'd been through enough this one night to last a lifetime.

A police officer stopped her at the door, trying to bar her entrance.

"I'm staying here. My name is Amelia Morgan and I'm a hosp—"

"Amelia!" Julia rushed to her, taking in her rain-soaked, bedraggled appearance. "Oh my God, what happened to you? Geoffrey is missing too, and we feared the worst."

Robert came up behind his wife, handing Amelia a blanket. "Wrap this around you for now. You must be freezing."

A man in a suit with a badge hanging from a lanyard introduced himself, "My name is Detective Hawkins. I take it you're the hospice nurse?"

Amelia nodded, "I am."

"We'd like you to answer some questions, but by the looks of it you would do better to change first. Would you meet us back in here?"

"Thank you." She gave him a grateful look. "I won't be long."

Julia fell in step with Amelia until the detective called out, "Mrs. Billings, I would appreciate it if you remained out here with the rest of us."

Julia stopped mid-step, looking at Amelia.

"I'll be fine," Amelia assured her.

She sent a prayer of thanks that the investigation was headed by a detective with common sense. Worried she'd be interrogated in a wet, clingy gown, she was grateful he'd given her leave to change into warmer clothes.

Amelia kept her word and took the fastest shower on record. Slipping on jeans and a thick cable-knit sweater, she made her way back to the living room.

Detective Hawkins nodded at her and pointed toward the sofa. As she sat down, he pulled up a chair alongside of her.

"Would you tell me what happened here tonight?" He flipped open a pad, ready to take notes. "I've already spoken to Mr. and Mrs. Billings. The coroner has been here, and Mrs. Marchand has been taken to the funeral home." He arched a brow as he pointed his pen at her. "I need you to fill in the holes for me, Ms. Morgan."

Amelia cleared her throat and began, filling the detective in on everything that had happened from when she left Ms. Audrey's room to get drinks to coming back from the cliffs. The only thing she omitted was Demetrius. She would never tell anyone about him. No one needed to know.

Detective Hawkins sat back after Amelia had finished.

"Given Geoffrey's background and past, I don't see you have anything to worry about. Mr. and Mrs. Billings vouch for you and speak very highly of you. I sent a team of men to search the beach for the body. Once the coroner pronounces cause of death, you will be free to go."

He rose but looked back at Amelia. "I would appreciate it if you would stay around a few more days, just until everything is cleared."

"Of course," Amelia agreed.

With Geoffrey gone, she wouldn't have a problem staying. Then again, Ms. Audrey was no longer here, so she wouldn't have anything to do either. One thing at a time.

When the police finally left, the cottage was eerily silent. The staff had long been back in their beds. Robert, Julia, and Amelia sat alone in the living room, sipping much-needed tumblers of whiskey.

Amelia didn't shy away from the burn of the liquor. She'd earned it tonight. Looking over at the couple on the sofa, Julia huddled against Robert, a huge pang of remorse filled her heart. Julia had lost her grandmother and her son on the same night.

"Julia?" When the woman looked her way, she added, "I'm so sorry about tonight, and everything that happened. If I could change anything..." Emotions and stress of the evening caught up to her and Amelia broke down, tears streaming down her cheeks. Pulling off her glasses, she tossed them onto the low table in front of her.

Arms wrapped her in a tight hug and Julia cried with her.

"My dear Amelia, none of this is your fault. I take all the blame for not telling you about Geoffrey. He should have never been allowed back in this house."

Amelia blinked up at her. "But he was your son—"

"He was a monster." Julia shuddered. "I should have let him go to prison instead of coddling him in a mental institution. He didn't deserve it." She clenched her hands together to stop the shaking. "I won't mourn his death, not for a minute. He will be cremated, and I'll dump his ashes in the ocean. I will save my grief for my grandmother."

"I'll miss Ms. Audrey." Amelia sighed. "She was a good lady."

"Yes, she was." Julia smiled at her. "I'm so glad you were here for her."

"Ladies, it's been a long night." Robert stood. "How about we get some rest? We'll have to be at the funeral home early to get everything finalized." He turned to Amelia. "Will you be all right here by yourself?"

"I'll be fine. I'm going to sleep in, then get my things together. Try to figure out what's next."

"You don't have to rush off. You're more than welcome to stay as long as you'd like," Julia offered.

"Thanks. I'll see where I land when the investigation is over."

CHAPTER 15

Amelia woke the next morning to sunlight streaming through the cracks of the drapes. Easing out of bed, she opened the curtains to find no traces of the horrible storm from the night before. Everything appeared washed clean, a new beginning in place.

Stretching, she planned how she would spend her day. Breakfast first, life decisions after.

Curious looks met her as she entered the kitchen, but no one said anything. They probably wanted to know about last night's events, but didn't ask, and she didn't offer. Amelia had told her version to Detective Hawkins and didn't want to talk about it anymore.

After a shower, Amelia went through Ms. Audrey's room and gathered all of her personal belongings. The room was different now with her patient gone. It was just one of many empty rooms in this huge mansion these people called a cottage. While she'd enjoyed her stay, she couldn't say she was going to miss anything about it.

As Amelia was packing things she wasn't going to need for the next few days, her cell phone rang. The familiar ringtone was one she hadn't heard much since she'd started the job. Her friends didn't call, instead texting or emailing her to see how she was doing. Glancing at the device, Demetrius' name flashed on the screen.

In a rush, all the horror of the night before slammed into her with conflicting emotions about Demetrius mixed in.

"Hello," she hesitantly answered.

There was a pause before Demetrius answered.

"I hear doubt in that one word, *mikros*. Have you changed your mind about me?"

How *did* she feel about him? Last night she'd seen the monster he truly was. He was capable of incredible violence, but it wasn't aimed at her. He'd protected her—he always would.

"No, I haven't, but we need to talk. Could you come pick me up? I don't want to go to the cliffs."

"I'll be there in ten minutes."

She ended the call, looking around at the room she'd called home for the last few months. She had a lot of decisions to make and didn't think there would be the luxury of time for some of them.

By the time she gathered her things and walked to the front door, Demetrius was parked outside. She slipped inside his car and he took off, neither one saying a word until he pulled up to his house.

"I figured this was the best place for us to talk. There won't be any interruptions."

She nodded as she entered the warmth of his house. The fireplace was going, just like the last time she'd been here. Everything looked the same, but yet so much had changed.

Amelia eased onto the sofa, grabbing a throw pillow to hold on to. Demetrius sensed her discomfort and didn't crowd her, sitting on the other end.

"Speak to me, Amelia. Tell me what's going through your mind. I need to know where we stand."

She forced herself to meet his gaze.

"That's just it. I don't know. I'm still trying to wrap my head around everything that's happened, everything you are..." She pulled off her glasses, rubbing the bridge of her nose. "It's not every day you're stalked by a psychopath and saved by a vampire." Her attempt at humor fell flat, and she blushed furiously. "I'm sorry, I don't even know what I'm saying anymore."

Demetrius moved closer, then caught himself, forcing himself to stay in place.

"I'm the one who's sorry. I should have never pursued you." He ran a hand through his thick hair. "But I can't help what I feel. Amelia, you are the purest soul I've ever known in my very long life. I'm drawn to you like a moth to a flame. Loving you has been the easiest and the hardest thing I've ever done. I'm sorry, but I have no regret."

Amelia's eyes filled with tears, but she refused to let them fall, furiously blinking them back.

"I'm scared, Demetrius. I love you, there's no doubt in my mind, but all the rest... I'm not sure. I don't know enough to decide."

This time, he moved closer, but only to take her hand in his.

"I'm not asking for more than what you can freely give. Stay with me, travel with me. Learn who I am and what it means to be vampire. I won't pressure you, I promise."

Could she do that? Could she be with him without becoming like him?

"A year?"

Demetrius tilted his head. "A year?"

"Yes," Amelia nodded, long curls bouncing around her shoulders. "Give me a year to make up my mind if I want to become like you."

"You will stay with me in that year?"

"I may want to work or go to school."

"Only if you will travel with me when you're free."

"So, basically, we would be living together as an exclusive couple, and I'll remain human."

Demetrius laughed loudly, the sound deep and hearty. It was the first time she'd ever heard him truly laugh. She liked it.

"*Agápi mou*, as long as you are sharing your life with me, I will agree to almost anything." His dark brown eyes turned serious. "There is one thing I would ask of you."

"What?" Amelia swallowed hard.

"Would you allow me to drink from you?" He added before she had the chance to turn him down, "You would not turn. I've told you before, I require little

124

sustenance because of my age. If you would allow me to drink from you, it would be all I would ever need."

Amelia couldn't deny the thought of it strangely excited her. His kisses tilted her world, what would this feel like?

She pulled him closer, he went willingly.

"Would you drink from me now?"

His eyes were liquid pools of chocolate rimmed with red.

"Are you sure?"

She nodded.

Demetrius cupped her face, kissing her gently, licking the seam of her lips until she moaned softly. Deepening the kiss, his tongue slipped inside, melding with hers. She was pliant and willing under his touch. Never had she been kissed like this.

He pushed her hair aside, exposing her neck. Amelia could feel her heart pounding. Demetrius' body tensed as he kissed the length of her neck, stopping at her carotid. He licked her slowly, then razor-sharp fangs pierced her skin. A flash of pain, then euphoria took over, filling her with an overwhelming sensual haze. He drank from her only a few times, then stopped. Licking the bite, he pulled her into his arms.

"Thank you, *mikros*. You have given me a priceless gift."

Looking up at him, she'd found her life's destiny.

Amelia closed her suitcase, standing it next to the door and the rest of her luggage. She was packed and ready to leave.

Audrey's funeral had been this morning with the service held at a church downtown, filled to capacity. The minister had given a moving sermon, then praised Audrey Marchand as a caring and generous woman, one who'd given much to the town and local charities. The funeral had been private, only the caretakers, Robert, Julia, and she had been allowed on the cliffs to see Audrey laid to rest in the crypt. For a moment, Amelia thought she'd seen Demetrius in the forest, but the trees were dense and shadowy.

Detective Hawkins had stopped by yesterday to let them know Geoffrey's death had been ruled as an accidental fall. Landing on jagged rocks, his back had broken, severing the spinal cord. Wild animals had torn him apart before the police had found the body.

Julia had ordered the cremation and to have the ashes dumped into the ocean. She wanted nothing more to do with her son.

Amelia had said her goodbyes to Julia and Robert a while ago. With promises to keep in touch, Julia had handed her a long manilla envelope.

"Grandmother's attorney asked me to give this to you. He figured you wouldn't want to hang around for the reading of Grandmother's will."

"What is it?" Curiosity and shock filled her as she accepted the envelope. With shaking hands, she opened it.

"Grandmother wanted you to take that photography course. She said you had an uncanny knack for detail. Grandmother always had a love for all forms of art. She used to sketch when she was younger," Julia explained, a tender smile on her face.

Amelia thought of the sketch tucked away in her suitcase. "She did like my photos." Amelia's knees threatened to buckle when she read the contents of the letter and the enclosed check.

"Oh my God!" Looking up at Julia, she exclaimed, "She left me $100,000!"

Julia smiled widely. "It should cover the course."

"And then some," Amelia added. "But I can't take this..."

"You can, and you will," Julia insisted. "It's what Grandmother wanted. She truly cared for you in the short time you were here. This is her way of showing you."

"Thank you, Amelia, for all you've done." Julia hugged her tightly, tears shining in her bright eyes. "Enjoy your life and make a difference."

"I'll do my best," she replied, as she wiped away her own tears.

CHAPTER 16

One year later, a villa overlooking the Aegean Sea

Amelia stared out over the sea, sunlight casting sparkles of diamonds on the calm surface. She still couldn't believe she was here, in Greece. Everything Demetrius had told her about his country had been true. Rich in history, its people were colorful and fascinating. She didn't want to leave, but then she'd said that about every country they'd visited so far.

Venice during Carnival had been exciting and romantic. Ireland had been fun, the cliffs were beautiful, and the pubs in Dublin had been an experience she wouldn't soon forget. The castles of Scotland were fairytale-like, and she'd admit freely to spending more than one night trying to spot the castle's ghosts. Egypt had been incredible, seeing the pyramids up close and riding camels were experiences she'd remember forever. Every place Demetrius had taken her had been an incredible adventure and a living history lesson. Her journey with Demetrius was only beginning.

Demetrius had kept his word. He'd given her the asked-for year. In that time, she'd worked, took several photography classes, traveled, and gotten to know him better. She'd learned what his life as a vampire had been like. Living a thousand years hadn't always been easy and he'd suffered greatly through the centuries. But he'd also lived with joy and experienced many amazing things. He'd seen so much of history in the making. Amelia wanted that. She wanted to experience all that life could offer.

"Amelia?"

She looked over her shoulder at Demetrius as he approached. His steps were silent, as usual. She wouldn't have known he was there if he hadn't called out her name.

"Is everything all right?"

"Of course, I was just enjoying the scenery. It's so beautiful and peaceful from here."

"Are you sure this is what you want?" Demetrius kissed her on the side of her neck, his hands sliding down to rest at her waist.

"We've been through this," Amelia replied, turning to face him, her arms wrapping around his neck. "You've explained everything to me dozens of times and I understand it all. I've been taking sips of your blood this past year to ensure the transition when it's time. You're going to drain me, I'll go to sleep, and when I wake up, I'll be a vampire."

"That's the simplified version, to be sure." Demetrius sighed.

"I'm the one who's going to be turned. Why are you so worried now?" Amelia demanded. "You said you wanted this."

He pulled her closer to him, stroking her long, silky hair.

"I want nothing more, *agápi mou*. This past year has been beyond bliss for me. Seeing the world through your eyes has made me see things I'd forgotten. I've never been happier. I just want to make sure this is what you truly want. There's no going back, *mikros*."

Meeting his gaze, his liquid brown eyes searched her blue ones for any signs of doubt. He wouldn't find any. He was right about one thing, this past year had been truly beyond bliss. She never dreamed she could be so happy. And now, she wanted to make sure it never ended.

"Were you able to find a descendant of the mage?"

"I did, and she's confident she can duplicate the tattoo and infuse it with the same spell. We'll just have to wait a few months before she does the work."

"Why do we have to wait?" Amelia asked. "I want to be able to walk in the sun with you."

Demetrius' eyes sparkled, and he chuckled.

"Remember, I told you the thirst is all-consuming at first. You will need to be able to control your hunger. We can't have you ripping out the mage's throat before she finishes the spell."

"I forgot about that." Amelia's eyes widened. "You're right. Can't take a chance." She looked out over the sparkling blue waters of the Aegean Sea. "You really think it will take that long before I can control the thirst?"

He held her tight, kissing her lightly.

"It depends entirely on the person. You're a very strong woman, my Amelia. I think you may surprise us both."

Demetrius led her to the bedroom, and together, they laid in the middle of the king-sized bed. He kissed her deeply, and Amelia melted against him, trusting him as she had trusted no other. When he pushed her hair back, she closed her eyes. The time had come.

"I love you, Demetrius. You've made me happier than I've ever been."

His eyes softened at her words.

"Our life together is only beginning."

His bite was ecstasy, bringing her to a plane of untold pleasure. He drank deeply, groaning his pleasure in her ear. She became lightheaded after a while and the urge to pull away grew stronger. Demetrius pulled her closer, drawing deeper from her life's blood, taking it all... until she slept.

"Awaken, *agápi mou.*"

Amelia slowly opened her eyes.

THE END

BEFORE YOU GO!

If you liked this book, please do me a huge favor and leave a review. Reviews are a small thing that mean so much to authors. They're invaluable as a means of advertising.

Leaving an Amazon review is like telling your friends you liked a book. After a book gets 20 reviews, Amazon suggests books in "also bought" and "you might like this" lists. This increases a book's visibility which boots sales.

After 50 to 75 reviews, Amazon highlights the book for spotlight positions for its newsletter. This is a HUGE boost for the author! Reviews help authors to sell more books.

An honest review is one of the most important things you can do to support an author. So, if you enjoyed this book, I'd be eternally grateful if you'd head over to Amazon, Goodreads, or BookBub and leave a review.

Thanks in advance!

ALSO BY MADISON GRANGER

Paranormal Romance

The Kindred Series

Phoenix Rising

Eternal Embrace

A Destiny Denied

Blindsided

Deuces Wild

Fated Journey (2021)

Stand-Alone

Save The Last Dance

Heart of Stone

Urban Fantasy

To Kill A Demon

PHOENIX RISING

Book One of The Kindred Series

———————

Madison Granger

CHAPTER 1

Torie conceded to two thoughts simultaneously; Christmas shopping was overrated, and the spirit of Christmas was dead, buried under a glittering blanket of commercialism. She'd never been a big fan of crowds. There were way too many people out and about this weekend for her liking. She was doing her best to forge through the masses to get the last elusive gift items on her list. Then there was the traffic. "Seriously! Does everyone think they have the only vehicle on the road?" she muttered. It seemed the streaming multitude left their IQ's and common sense at home. If she made it to her house in one piece, she would consider herself a holiday shopper survivor.

Torie parked her SUV, sighing with resignation for the things she couldn't control. Grabbing her cell phone, keys, and purse, she headed across the full parking lot to the local bookstore. She'd been out all morning and most of the afternoon in search of Christmas presents for friends. Usually, she shopped online, but sometimes you just had to get out and fight the crowds for that *perfect* gift. Unfortunately, those *perfect* gifts were getting harder and harder to find, or someone else had the same idea and by the time Torie got to the shelf, they were already gone. Frustration was rearing its ugly head. She'd come to the realization that she needed an indulgence break before continuing her search. A book for herself and a shot of caffeine should brace her for the rest of the shopping day.

Entering The Literal Word, she was regaled with bright lights, colorful displays, and Christmas music playing over the speakers. Torie loved this store. She delighted in the convenience of shopping online, but there was nothing like browsing aisles and shelves of books.

Here, she was in her element. Books were her comfort zone, her friend, and her solace when she needed mental pampering. As she glanced around the setup, Torie took in the crowd browsing for books or the latest book-related gadget. There were plenty of them. People were running into each other trying to get through narrow passages to look at all the items.

Java Joe's, the in-house coffee shop, was also catering to a maximum crowd. Wistfully, Torie wondered if she would be able to get a cappuccino after she'd made her purchases. Slinging her bag up on her shoulder, she navigated to her favorite section. A romance book with a sexy werewolf or vampire was always a welcome escape from her busy, but lonely life. An auburn-haired, green eyed middle-age divorcee, Torie was a graduate of the *been there, done that, have a drawer full of t-shirts* school of life. After so many failed relationships, she was pretty sure the rest of her life was going to be spent alone. Being on the more-than-curvy side pretty much insured it. Men her age seemed to all want that pretty, young trophy type on their arm. *It is what it is* had become her mantra.

It wasn't a bad life, in itself. Torie had family, a brother and sister. She also had a grown daughter and a precocious granddaughter she adored. She had a job she liked, and made a decent living, too. There just wasn't a special man in her life. That kind of loneliness was hard for her. It had been a long time since there had been anyone memorable. Torie missed the best parts of a relationship, the companionship, sharing of ideas and thoughts, laughter, and the sex. *Yeah, I miss the sex.* Shaking her head ruefully, she berated herself for the pity party. That kind of thinking was depressing and never got her anywhere. It was time to shove it back into that tiny compartment in her brain and try, once again, to forget about it.

Approaching the Paranormal Romance section, Torie noticed they'd added a tier of shelves right before it of New Releases. *Well, this makes it a little easier to find what I'm looking for.* Browsing through the titles, she scanned for releases by her favorite authors first. Torie picked up a few unknowns and started reading the back covers to find her next book boyfriend. After selecting a couple that seemed promising, she ambled over to another section of her favored genres, Science Fantasy. There was one book that had been released recently. She wondered if it was on the shelf yet, or if she would have to order it.

When she got to the section, Torie spotted her goal on a lower shelf. *Naturally! Why do they have to put them way down there?* Bending down, she grabbed the book. As she straightened, she lost her balance and faltered side to side, dropping everything. Her purse too, fell off her shoulder, landing on the floor. Reddening with embarrassment, Torie bent down to retrieve her goods with a muttered oath. A man's strong, long-fingered hand came into her line of vision, reaching for her books as Torie grabbed her purse.

"Allow me," entreated an amused deep voice. He held her arm, lending her his support so she could stand.

Flustered beyond belief, still blushing furiously, Torie peered up to thank the man for his kindness. She gazed into the most mesmerizing pair of sky-blue eyes she'd ever seen. Torie found herself struck dumb. She took in his shaved head, a handsome face with a sexy soul patch under his bottom lip, and a drop-dead killer smile. She finally managed to stammer, "Tha . . . thank you."

He smiled back at her. "Always a pleasure to assist a lady in distress."

The handsome stranger held the books out to her. Torie, regaining her composure, reached up to take them back into her arms. She couldn't help but notice how very tall he was. She looked up to give him a grateful smile. His tailored slacks and button-down shirt did nothing to disguise the definition of his well-sculpted body. The rolled sleeves partially covered what appeared to be a full sleeve of tribal tattoos on his right arm. *Oh my, this guy is the stuff fantasies are made of.*

His gaze went from her arms loaded with books to making eye contact. "Have you found everything you are looking for?" His smile, devastatingly sexy, was aimed right at her. Her heart went into overdrive. It'd been ages since she found herself attracted to any man, and here was her proverbial *sex on a stick,* talking to *her.* She said a quick prayer not to flub this. "Yes, as far as shopping for books goes, I'm pretty well done."

"In that case," he started in a low pitched, husky voice, "could I interest you in a coffee?"

Torie double-checked to see if he was indeed serious in his offer. The expression on his face seemed sincere. There was no way she was going to pass up on this chance to find out who this gorgeous guy was. Her mouth curved into a smile. "I'd love some coffee. Thanks. Let me pay for my books first, and I'll meet you there."

Sweeping an arm out toward the front of the store, he motioned for her to go first. As she turned to go to the registers, he added, "I shall wait for you here."

Throwing him a quick smile, she got in line hoping it wouldn't take long to pay for her books.

For once, they had enough employees behind the counters. Checkout went quickly and she met up with him. Walking toward the coffee shop, her handsome Good Samaritan leaned toward her. "What kind of coffee would you like?"

Torie always got flustered trying to make decisions at these coffee places. There were so many to choose from and she never could decide what she wanted. Everyone else always seemed to know exactly what they desired all the time. The man asking the question now upped the ante. Looking up at the lighted sign on the wall, she noticed the highlighted special. Crossing her fingers that it was a decent choice, she answered, "The Spiced Gingerbread Cappuccino sounds interesting."

Walking to the counter to place their orders, he turned back to her. "Would you mind getting a table for us? I will be there shortly with our coffees."

As Torie glanced around the crowded room, her gaze locked on a table that was being vacated. She hurried over, cleaned up after the couple who'd left everything behind, and disposed of the trash. In the few minutes she had to wait for the handsome stranger to join her, she tried to regain her composure and get her act together. *She was acting like a schoolgirl, for crying out loud.* It had been such a long time since she had any social interaction with a man, she was sorely out of practice and nervous. As he neared the table, she once again marveled at him. He was drop-dead gorgeous. This stranger was everything she'd ever fantasized about when it came to the perfect man. Now she would find out if his personality matched the outside. She sighed. *A woman could only hope.*

He carefully placed their coffees on the table and sat across from her. The table and chairs weren't small, yet he seemed to dwarf everything around him. Not only was he a big man, his presence seemed to add *more* to his already dominating size. With a heart-melting smile, he introduced himself. "My name is Quinn McGrath, and you are?"

Flustered by his sensuous smile, Torie bit her lip before returning the introduction. "I'm Torie Masters.

Thank you for the coffee . . . and again for your help earlier."

"Not a problem, believe me. I am glad I was in the right place at the right time."

To her relief, their conversation went smoothly. She'd never been very good at chatting. He kept the conversational flow going by asking questions and listening intently to her answers. Torie discovered that Quinn, like her, was an avid reader. He preferred mysteries and a little science fiction, having several favorite authors in both genres. From books, they ventured to movies and music. She was continually surprised at how much they had in common. The conversation between them flowed easily and the banter was light and casual, making the time pass quickly.

When Torie heard her phone chime with a text, she checked it hastily. She'd heard the faint chime a couple of times before but had ignored it. She'd been enjoying her conversation too much to want to be interrupted. Figuring her daughter was going to be persistent until she replied, she tapped out a quick answer. Looking at the clock on the face of her phone, she was astonished to find that more than two hours had passed. She noticed a slight look of disappointment flitting across Quinn's handsome face as she checked the messages. She looked up when he enquired, "Do you have to go?"

"No, not at all. My daughter is checking on me. I'm not usually out this long," she confessed.

"Excellent. Could I persuade you to have dinner with me? I am enjoying your company and I really am not ready for our time together to end."

Torie's initial reaction was to thank him politely and decline the invitation, but she hesitated. Here was an uber attractive man who seemed genuinely interested in her. They had spent the last two hours caught up in captivating conversation. *Why **not** have dinner with him? What could it possibly hurt?* It had been way too long since she'd enjoyed the company of a man. She was going to do this.

Quinn must have understood her hesitancy. When she didn't respond immediately, he added, "I realize we do not know each other yet. There is a steak house right across the parking lot, we can walk over there to have dinner. You will not be far from your vehicle." He placed his hand over hers briefly. "Would that make you feel a little more secure?"

Didn't that just seal the deal? "I would really like that. Thank you." She accepted his invitation with a gracious smile.

Quinn cleared away their coffee cups. Coming back to the table, he reached for her purchases. "Would you like to put these in your vehicle before we go to the restaurant?"

Feeling like he was reading her mind, she readily agreed. "That would be great. My truck is right out front."

With a hand on the small of her back, Quinn escorted her out of the bookstore and to her SUV. She stashed her bag in the back with her other purchases before making sure it was locked. They walked through the still full parking lot over to Vincent's Restaurant. It was one of her favorite places to eat. The aroma of grilled steaks and freshly baked bread filled the air, greeting them before they reached the door.

Entering the dimly lit crowded eatery threw Torie's assaulted senses into overload. The dining area echoed with laughter, music, plates clanging, and murmured conversations. Trying to acclimate to the soft lighting and not get crushed by the crowd was a challenge. Quinn took charge immediately, using his body to protect her from the hordes of people rushing around them. He put an arm around her shoulders, drawing her close. It was all Torie could do not to melt right into Quinn's side. *He's so very strong . . . and rock solid . . . and his scent . . . what was that? Sandalwood, Sage, both? It was glorious, whatever it was.* She wanted to stay right where she was, drinking him in.

Quinn flashed a charming smile at the hostess, and they were quickly led to their seats. Torie wondered how that happened so fast, considering there was a group of people standing around the entrance, obviously on a wait list. She saw the young woman beaming up at Quinn, trying her best to be flirtatious. Torie smiled to herself. She couldn't blame the attendant for trying. If it got them a table, then more power to her and Quinn. Pulling out a chair for her, Quinn waited until she settled in her seat before walking around the table to take his own chair. He ran his hand lightly over Torie's shoulders as he walked by. *Brownie points for manners.* She indulged in an inward thrill at his touch, grateful she hadn't been wearing a jacket or coat that would have hampered the feel of his caress. As much as she enjoyed colder weather, the winters in southern Louisiana were usually mild.

"Is this to your liking?" asked Quinn, pulling her from her thoughts.

"Yes, it's fine," she replied, still amazed at how quickly they had been seated.

A server came up immediately to take their drink orders, leaving them for a few minutes to go over their menus, and make their choices. Finding out how akin their preferences were in other areas, it wasn't all that surprising to discover they had similar tastes in food and how it was prepared. The conversation quickly picked up where it had left off at the bookstore. She found out that he was a financial consultant and owned his own business, McGrath Consulting. His brother, who had a corporate law background, was his partner. Quinn was looking for office space in the New Orleans and surrounding areas which had led him to Torie's hometown.

Their conversation paused when the server returned with their meals. As the food was placed in front of them, Quinn assured the server that everything was fine, and the young man left them to enjoy their meal. Resuming their talk, Quinn questioned her about her job. Torie was a little abashed to admit she was just a receptionist. He was quick to quash the *just* part of her job description. When he spoke to her, she felt like she was important, that what she did counted. Torie knew he was right. She did a lot more than simply answer phones and take messages, though seldom did anyone think of it that way, especially her boss.

Over their meal, Quinn regaled her with stories of his childhood in Scotland. Torie was fascinated. She'd always dreamed of visiting Scotland but didn't think she would ever get the chance to travel. He had a way of telling stories that took her there, making her visualize the lovely scenery and the antics of two young brothers growing up in the Highlands.

"I have to say, for growing up in Scotland you don't have much of an accent," she observed between bites.

Quinn nodded. "It is true. It has faded over time. I have been away from Scotland for many years now. I have traveled the world over, several times. When you have had as many business dealings as I have with people of different cultures you tend to lose the accent. Aiming a disarming smile her way he added in a thick Scottish brogue, "Dinna fash yirsel lassie. Ah kin pull it oot whin a'm needin' it." He capped it off by throwing her a roguish wink.

"Yes indeed, you can. It's still there." Torie laughed in delight.

Later, lingering over coffee after their meal, Torie glanced around the room. It dawned on her that only a few patrons remained. "I guess we better call it a night. They'll be closing on us pretty soon."

Quinn reluctantly agreed. "Time seems to have gotten away from me today. I will walk you back to your vehicle." They wound their way through the tables, to make their way outside. Taking her hand, Quinn escorted Torie back to her truck. "Is there a chance I can see you tomorrow? I do not wish to rush you, but there is a reason for my asking."

Torie regarded him quizzically. "What do you mean?"

"I am going to be out of town for the next two weeks on business. I have really enjoyed my time with you today and I want to see you again before I have to leave," Quinn explained. "Please say yes."

"How can I possibly say no to that?" she asked, smiling brightly.

"Excellent!" Quinn replied with a broad grin. "Lunch, then?"

Laughing, Torie nodded. "Lunch, it is."

After exchanging phone numbers, Torie got into her SUV. In her rearview mirror, she could see Quinn stand in place as he watched her drive off, then slowly walk to his own car.

Torie drove home in a daze. *Who knew that today would be the stuff dreams were made of?* Parking her truck under the carport, she heard the chime that let her know she had a text message. Glancing down at her cell phone, she saw it was from Quinn.

Thank you for today. I look forward to seeing you tomorrow. ~Q.

Hugging herself, she knew she was going to have the most pleasant of dreams that night.

HEART OF STONE

———————

Madison Granger

PROLOGUE

Limoges, France—1545

Roul plunged deep one last time into the warm slickness of the wench's ample charms. He rolled off with a heaving grunt, fighting to draw in a breath. She was a lusty maid. He'd been enjoying her sensuous bounty for a fortnight now. Roul knew better than to continue letting her into his bed, but she was more than a passing good tumble. Besides, he would have to leave the manor to find someone else to take her place. That was more energy than it was worth, as he was tired of the city, the politics, and the social pressure.

Bussing her soundly on her sensually pliant lips, he swatted her round bottom. "Off with you now. I have an appointment with my father and he hates to be kept waiting."

Giggling, she slid off the bed and reached for her chemise. She cupped her generous breasts, offering them with a simper. "Are you sure I can't talk you into another go, milord?"

He shot her a roguish wink, then turned to pull his breeches on. "I'm afraid not, tout-petit. Duty calls. Now, hurry on before you're seen."

She gave a moue of disappointment but did as she was bid. Lacing her skirt in place, she eased out of his bedchamber, pausing to check for onlookers before she scampered down the hall.

Adjusting his linen shirt to lay smoothly, Roul glanced at his reflection in the mirror. Presentable enough he surmised, hastening to meet his father downstairs.

Roul hesitated in the doorway of the office. When his father glanced up and motioned him in, Roul strode to the wingback facing the huge mahogany desk. Easing his length into the chair, he patiently waited while his father finished writing. Roul glanced around the familiar room. Elegant furniture graced the large area and custom-made rugs covered the tiled floors. Books filled most of the ceiling-to-floor bookshelves, with the occasional souvenir from vast travels posing as a focal point. As the Earl d'Aguessean, his father traveled extensively, always bringing back treasures for himself and his family. Roul had always loved this room, having spent many an evening as a child playing in front of the fireplace while his father poured over the estate's records.

He studied his father from under hooded lids. Etienne Jourdan, the current Earl, still cut an impressive figure. The man was in good health, and with luck, would continue to enjoy his title for a long time yet to come. This meeting wasn't the norm, and Roul was curious to learn what had brought it about. When his father pushed back from the desk, he figured he was about to find out.

"I'm glad you found time to meet with me, son. I hope I didn't interrupt too much with your current dalliance."

Roul had the grace to duck his head, his cheeks staining a ruddy hue. "You asked for a meeting, mon père. Of course, I will meet you whenever you wish."

"You have always been a dutiful son. No matter where your current hobbies lie." Etienne studied his firstborn, seeming to measure his worth with a glance. "I called you here to let you know that your mother and I have deemed it time for you to marry. We have made the arrangements. You will meet your bride-to-be this weekend."

He swallowed hard, not believing he'd heard correctly. His chest constricted, and he felt the blood rushing to his head. "My marriage, mon père? But I am only twenty and five. Surely there is no reason to rush into an arrangement?"

The Earl stepped over to a set of double doors alongside a long wall. Opening them, he motioned to Roul. "Come, let's walk in the garden. We'll talk more outside."

Roul was stunned to his core. Marriage. He was not ready for this but knew better than to cause a scene. He needed to gather his wits about him, presenting a calm and convincing argument. Surely, he could talk his father out of his decision. At the very least, put it off for a time.

He walked alongside his father. For the first time, he was unaware of the beauty surrounding him. His mother had turned the garden into a show piece. He'd spent countless pleasant hours with her admiring the colorful blooms while they visited. Now, the brilliant colors seemed to pale beside his father's distressing announcement. Roul had to force himself to focus.

His father was speaking, and he'd missed what had been said. "I'm sorry, Papa, what was that?"

Etienne came to a stop, placing a comforting hand on Roul's shoulder. "It truly isn't a terrible thing, mon fils. The Viscount's daughter is a very attractive young woman. She has been schooled in all the niceties of society. I have been told she is an intelligent creature. She should make you a fine wife. She comes with a generous dowry, too." He searched his son's eyes. "It is time for you to assume responsibility, Roul. I ask that you meet with her. Be your charming self. I'm sure once you meet her, you will feel an attraction."

Roul spent a few more minutes with his father, discussing trivial matters. When he could finally make his excuses, he strode to his chambers. He wanted to change clothes and head to the stables. Maybe a good, long gallop would clear his head, or at the very least, allow him to think.

Roul pulled the stallion to a halt. Upon hearing the heavy breathing of his mount, he immediately felt guilty for taking his frustrations out on the poor beast. He'd worked the horse into a lather trying to run from his problems. He reined the horse in to a slow walk, allowing him to cool down naturally. He made a mental note to tend to him personally when he returned to the stables.

His gaze wandered over the vineyards to the south of their property. Their family had done well financially between the bounty of the arbors and the cattle peacefully grazing in the pastures to the east of the manor. He had a good life. Roul didn't consider himself a total rake, but he admitted to enjoying the pleasures of being a bachelor of means. He wasn't ready to assume the responsibility of marriage and family.

With a tightening of his legs, he urged the horse toward the stables. He'd promised his father he would meet the Viscount's daughter. It would make his parents happy, giving him time to figure a way around the dilemma.

Saturday morning burst through Roul's bedchamber windows. He groaned as the sunlight pierced his eyelids, forcing himself to push the coverlet aside. Camille, the Viscount's daughter would be here soon. He wanted to be presentable and fortify himself with a decent meal before she arrived. He had a feeling he wouldn't have much of an appetite as the day progressed.

He went through his ablutions automatically, dressing quickly. His breeches fit snugly against his muscular thighs, and his knee-high boots shone with a high polish. The linen shirt was form fitting, snugging against his well-defined chest. It wasn't proper attire for court, but he was at home, and he meant to dress as was his wont. The Honourable Camille would just have to deal with his eccentricities.

Roul was chatting with his father in the office when a servant announced the arrival of a carriage. He inwardly sighed, making his way to the front of the manor to meet his intended. A shudder escaped him at the thought. Please let this day go by swiftly, he prayed. Squaring his shoulders and plastering on a polite smile, he approached the two women. The Viscount's wife and daughter slowly made their way toward him and his father. He admitted that the young woman was attractive in a pale, insipid manner. Flaxen-haired and adorned in pastel colors, she was almost colorless in contrast to his tanned skin, wavy ebony hair, and dark-brown eyes. While her figure was attractive, her appearance left him lacking. He found himself hoping she could hold an intelligent conversation, or this weekend would prove to be his undoing.

After polite conversation, he invited Camille to view his mother's garden. Maybe there, they could find common ground to bridge their differences.

Surprisingly, the Viscount's daughter was not only intelligent, but quite articulate. Conversing with her proved no hardship, and he found himself laughing at a small tale she wove regarding her brother.

The day passed quickly. A family luncheon, then dinner, found him relaxing and enjoying his visit with Camille. Maybe, in time, he could bring himself to have feelings for the lady. It wouldn't be the worst thing to happen to him. Once the ladies retired for the evening, he poured himself a tumbler of his father's best scotch and slipped outside to the garden. Lost in thought, he didn't hear the rustle of a skirt until the slip of a girl faced him.

"Is it true, milord?"

Startled by the maid's sudden appearance, he stopped short. "Excuse me?" He quickly glanced around before continuing. "What are you doing out here?"

Tears filled her eyes as she gazed up at him. "Is it true, milord? Are you to marry the Viscount's daughter?"

Puzzled, he kept his counsel. He wasn't raised to be discourteous to the servants, but there were boundaries, and he was perplexed as to why this chit thought she could question him. Inwardly he groaned— he'd known he should've curtailed his romps with her. Dalliances with the help never proved wise.

"I don't believe that should concern you in any way, Marie. But I will relent this once and tell you that arrangements like these are a common occurrence. The Honourable Camille may indeed become my intended."

He thought he'd handled things as diplomatically as possible. Most would have sent her scurrying on her way with nary a word.

The petite maid's face drew up tight in anger. "You would marry that . . . that pasty-faced, prissy woman? What about us? What about the pleasure I give you?"

He nearly spat out the drink in shock at her outburst. "Here now, girl, you go too far."

She slapped him. Hard. "I shall go farther still. You have a heart of stone, and for that you shall pay the price. I curse you." She spat on the ground and stomped her foot, grinding the toe of her slipper into the ground. "I curse you to a life that matches your heart. For five hundred years you will live as stone, cold as the heart which beats in your chest. You will be bound to stone by day, and by night you will guard the very ones who mean so little to you. Release will only come when you receive the unconditional love of a mortal woman. If you do not find love, you will remain in stone forever." Her face twisted into a snarl. "No woman will love a monster such as you. Prepare yourself for an eternity of loneliness!"

He felt a surge of energy crash into him. The air slowly left his lungs, and he struggled to breathe. In horror, he watched as his normally tanned arm paled, taking on a gray pallor. He fell to the ground on one knee, his body slowly stiffening. Roul struggled, but movement was no longer an option. His anguished cries crashed inside his head but were heard by no one. Within minutes, a life-size statue of a winged gargoyle, crouched upon one knee, graced the garden of the Countess d'Aguessean.

CHAPTER 1

Bellerieve, Louisiana—Present Day

Lexi bit her lip as she replayed the last few hours at work. The unimaginable had happened. She'd been fired. She knew the boss' niece had been hired simply to placate his sister. Lexi never dreamed the little hussy would not only want Lexi's position, but would manage to get rid of her as well. She threw herself in the chair, groaning. The chair squeaked in protest at the rough treatment. She massaged her temple with one hand, fighting to hold back the impending tears. She'd never been fired from any job before. Her confidence and self-esteem had taken a horrific blow. Now what was she going to do?

Jobs weren't easy to come by. Degrees and diplomas didn't ensure job positions, especially these days, and in her locale. The oilfield industry in south Louisiana was at an all-time low, and it affected every aspect of the job stream.

She gazed out the window, not seeing anything. Sunlight poured in through the sheer, mint-colored curtains, but she was oblivious to the cheery spot she claimed as her personal space. Her mind reeled, playing back the scene over and over. In the matter of a few weeks, Heather had her uncle believing that Lexi was not doing her job and stealing supplies from the office as well. The kicker had been when Lexi found some magazines in her desk drawer. Obviously not hers, she was about to throw them in the trash when Heather and her uncle walked in. Right then, Heather pointed them out and accused her of wasting the company's time and money. Stunned, Lexi was speechless. She'd worked there for over five years, and her record was impeccable. But her boss didn't seem to care. He called her in and cut her loose, right then and there.

Reality was sinking in. She was without a job. She had rent and bills to pay. Jobs were scarce. What was she going to do now? Her bottom lip quivered, tears streaming down her cheeks. Lexi was alone, she had no one to turn to. She had friends, and they would be sympathetic, but that's not what she needed. She needed a miracle. Unfortunately, her luck didn't run that route. She was more the *if it weren't for bad luck, I'd have no luck at all* type.

She heaved a sigh, shuffling morosely to the kitchen. Lexi ran a hand through short, strawberry-blonde tresses, reaching for a mug with the other one. She needed coffee. Caffeine fortification on the highest level, and lots of it. With liquid nirvana in hand, she sat at her computer to begin the tedious process of searching for another job. It was going to be a long night.

Stretching and groaning, harsh reality hit in a wave, and Lexi covered her head with the sheet. She didn't want to get up, but she knew she wouldn't be able to stay in bed, either. Swinging her legs over the side of the mattress, she ran her fingers through her hair. She was more tired right this second than when she went to bed hours ago. She had a feeling that was a sign of her immediate future. Up until the wee hours of the morning, she'd updated her resume, and searched every job site she could think of. She'd lost count of how many applications she'd filled out. Lexi could only hope that something came through quickly. Her savings were meager at best, and wouldn't see her through very long.

Stumbling to the kitchen, she grabbed a mug and started the brewer. Coffee first, thinking next. *That was a plan, right?* Leaning against the counter, she crossed her legs at the ankles, contemplating a plan of action. She huffed out a breath of air. There wasn't much she could do today. Weekends were out as far as job hunting. She'd pretty much hit all the job searches online last night, applying for anything that came close to something she was qualified for. She'd even gone through the lengthy process to file for unemployment.

She fought back tears, burying her face in open hands. She felt tossed out like yesterday's garbage. Angrily wiping away her tears, she opened the faucet, splashing cool water on her face. Enough with the pity party. What's done was done, and it was what it was. Tears weren't going to accomplish anything.

Coffee mug in hand, she crossed the small space to her desk. Slowly swinging side to side in her chair, she nursed her drink and stared at her monitor. Emails and social media could wait, she wasn't in the mood to deal with any of it. Turning to face the window, she contemplated the outside world. It was a gorgeous day, clear blue skies mocking her dark mood. If she were smart, she'd dress and go out. Do something, do anything. It had to be better than sitting in her apartment, feeling sorry for herself.

One phone call later, and Lexi was already feeling better. She aimed her SUV down the busy highway, maneuvering toward the Starbucks closest to her apartment. Bethany promised to meet her at the coffee house in thirty minutes. She needed some best friend one-on-one. By the time Lexi weaved through the traffic, she would arrive at the designated time. If nothing else, she was punctual. Her best friend, however, was her polar opposite. Bethany was always late, so Lexi would have more than enough time to order their coffees and grab a table. Easing into a spot, she crossed the parking lot, glancing around for her best friend's vehicle. Not here yet. She smiled to herself.

There were a few things in life you could always count on, Bethany running late was one of them.

Ordering a Coconut milk Mocha Macchiato for Bethany and a Cappuccino for herself, she waited at the end of the counter for her drinks. She watched in fascination as the young barista managed to take orders and deftly put the complicated drinks together. She smiled to herself. Not a job she would be applying for. While she could multi-task with the best of them, she was sure this type of work would drive her up the wall. The downside to getting older, she supposed. With a grateful smile, she took her drinks from the young girl, and turned to secure a table. Finding a free one against the front window, she sat down to wait for her friend.

Lexi watched people going about their day as she sipped on her coffee. Saturdays were always pretty busy in this area. Shopping and other errands seemed to be the norm on weekends for most folks. This particular strip of road held nothing but shops and restaurants. Weekends found traffic more heavily congested than on normal workdays.

The door opened, and a flash of platinum blonde hair caught Lexi's attention. Large brown eyes locked on her, and Bethany gave her a broad wink as she wound her way through the tables to meet her. Sliding into her chair, she groaned. "Traffic sucks this morning. Guess everybody decided to go shopping." She took a sip of her coffee, eyes rolling in pleasure. "Geez, this stuff is pure ambrosia. Thanks."

Lexi grinned at her friend, sitting back with her own coffee in hand. She knew better than to try to say anything just yet. Bethany was a force to be reckoned with on a good day. After listing all her complaints about the traffic and the everyday habits of the masses, she plunked her cup on the small table, staring Lexi down.

"Okay, give." She waved her hands before Lexi could say a word. "I know what you told me on the phone. I get that. He turned out to be a pain in the ass of a boss, anyway. No loss there. What are your plans now?"

She winced, stared out the window, then brought her gaze back to her friend's unblinking stare. She felt the tears threaten, fighting to hold them back. She let out a frustrated moan. "Haven't had time to make any plans." She shrugged, then took a sip of coffee. Placing it on the table she continued, "I filed for unemployment. If I'm lucky, it'll go through. I applied for everything I could find, not that there were a lot of openings. I'm just going to keep looking until I find something." She straightened, meeting Bethany's gaze. "What else is there?"

Bethany gave her a sympathetic smile. "Well, at least you're being proactive. I'm sure you'll find something soon enough. I'll keep my eyes and ears open for anything. I'll make a few calls on Monday, see if anyone has any openings. I know you don't want to, but if worse comes to worse, you can always move in with me." Bethany gave her a knowing look. "The offer's there if you want it." She finished off her coffee and rubbed her hands together. "So, what are we going to do today?"

Lexi loved her best friend more than anyone else in the world. She knew how hard Lexi had fought for her independence from a very controlling mother. Moving out of her apartment was going to be a last resort. Turning her thoughts to Bethany's question, she shrugged. This was the very reason she'd called her friend in the first place. Bethany would keep her busy, not letting her dwell on depressing thoughts. Grinning, she shook her head. "I'm obviously out of ideas. No money to shop, things are going to be tight for now. Suggestions?"

The blonde winked. "Got you covered, girlfriend. Let's drop off that tank you call a ride at your place. We're going on a road trip."

TO KILL A DEMON

The Chronicles of Sully and Larke

⇔

A Daemon's Desire

_____

Madison Granger

CHAPTER 1

Crouched and motionless on the ledge, Sully stared into the inky blackness of the scrying pool. He might have been mistaken for a stone statue, until his scarlet leathery wings unfurled, then settled against his muscular back once again. Standing, he stretched to his towering height of eight feet, canting his head towards the still waters. Those damnable demons were at it again. He was going to have to check it out.

It was his job to protect mankind from demons, the degree of difficulty being daemons and demons pretty much looked alike, making it hard to tell who the bad guys were. Of course, the daemons and demons knew the difference. It was the humans who had trouble with the scorecard.

Sighing heavily, he headed for the portal. Sully stood transfixed, staring at the swirling vaporous cloud which would transport him from his dimension to Earth's surface. Though the portal was painless and almost instantaneous, there was a fleeting moment of his body fracturing into a million components and being swept away that was just a tad disconcerting. After fifteen hundred years, you would think he would be used to it by now. Oh well, thinking about it wasn't going to change anything. Trudging one heavy boot after the other, he walked through the swirl, and vanished in a blink.

Materializing into an alley, he glanced around quickly. Seeing no one, he threw up glamour, allowing him to change his appearance to an acceptable nature for the time and place should anyone approach. He could disguise some of his height but was still imposing at 6' 8" in human form. Long black hair sat in waves around massive shoulders, and frosty green eyes stared out from a strong chiseled face outlined by a trimmed beard. A black tee stretched taut across a muscular chest that tapered down to leathers encasing strong well-built thighs. Combat boots completed the trappings for his stint on this plane. Snapping his fingers, a leather jacket appeared in his hand and he shrugged it on. Another snap, and two wicked looking daggers appeared. Ancient markings on the blades spoke of magical beginnings, and he slid them into compartments in the jacket.

Tilting his head, he listened. Not hearing anyone approaching, he made his way out of the alley and started walking towards the downtown district. Nightfall wasn't far off. He would find the ones he was searching for soon enough. As was the norm when he patrolled, people tended to find an excuse to duck off into buildings or cross the street when they saw him approach. He was intimidating and he knew it. Most of the time, it worked in his favor. It wouldn't do him any good if the demons he hunted saw him as weak, and therefore no threat, but just once he wished, just once, he would find someone he didn't strike terror in at first glance. A corner of his lip curled, and he snarled low and deep. What in the Seven Levels was he thinking anyway? Daemons weren't meant for happy ever afters. He was created for one purpose, to destroy demons. There was nothing else. He had never heard of anything else, anyway. Not that daemons were a very social lot. They answered to the Council, but for the most part, they tried to stay off of their radar, too. No sense in asking for trouble.

The sound of a woman crying out, and men laughing up ahead pulled him from his thoughts. He focused on the voices until he was able to pinpoint their location. Striding in their direction, he homed in on the voices once more. Two, no, three men laughing and threatening the woman. She was crying, begging for mercy, offering them money, anything... just let her go. He stealthily approached them. They had her pinned against a brick wall, effectively blocking her from getting away. One of them held a switchblade and was toying with her, a nick here to draw a little blood, a well-placed slice to garments to expose fleshy delights. The largest of the three unzipped his pants and walked towards her, stroking his erection while he licked his lips leering at her. When she saw the size of his member, she screamed and tried to fight them off. One of them grabbed and held her while Mr. Switchblade ripped what was left of her shirt down the middle, leaving her heaving breasts exposed to their appreciative glances. When he reached for a taut nipple, an ominous voice split the dusky evening, "I think that's about as far as you guys are going to go with this one."

All three of them turned, never letting go of the woman. Sully stood at the alley entrance, long muscled legs spread apart, formidable daggers in each hand. In a menacing guttural voice, the largest of the group spoke, "Back off daemon! This is none of your concern."

Sully arched a brow, and folded his arms across his chest, daggers held casually in each large hand, "Now you see, that's where you're wrong." He moved a step in their direction and they pulled the woman in front of them, using her as a shield. She threw a frightened look at Sully but made no sound. Tears trickled down her cheeks, and her eyes pled with him for help. "This is the kind of thing that is exactly my concern," he told them nonchalantly.

The one with the blade swished it menacingly and threatened, "We'll kill the human. Doesn't matter to us. We just wanted a little fun for starters." Pulling the woman back closer against him, the blade slid across her throat. A slow trickle of blood dripped from where he cut her. The woman moaned but didn't fight.

Sully shook his head, "You guys just don't get it." Leveling his gaze on the three, frigid green eyes bored into them. Before they could register he had moved, he threw both daggers. One hit the demon with the switchblade between the eyes, its twin taking out another one by the throat. That left Big Dick. Sully flashed in and swept the feet out from the remaining demon. As he lost his balance, Sully yanked him by his hair and with a vicious twist, snapped his neck. The woman fell to the ground in a faint. Sparing her a glance, a thought quickly crossed his mind, *"That was probably for the best."*

Within moments, the two demons who had been hit with the daggers disintegrated into small clouds of dust and smoke. Reaching for the knives, Sully wiped the blade of one and returned it to his jacket, before he used the other to slit the throat of the third demon. He wiped the blade clean on the demon's pants just as, and like his partners, he too faded away into dust and smoke.

Sully approached the woman and knelt before her. Placing a large hand on her forehead, he sifted through her memories. Able to find out her address, and that she had no one waiting at home for her, he lifted her easily into his arms. Glancing up at the now dark skies, he dropped his glamour, returned to his daemon form, and let his wings unfurl to their full span. Leaping into the air, he gained altitude and flew towards the woman's house. Luckily, it was in a small and quiet neighborhood. The front yard was comprised of a myriad of plants, bushes and flowers. Her back yard had a covered patio. He landed there.

Placing her in the chaise, he stepped back and observed her. Usually, he simply erased their memories and gave them new ones. It wasn't going to account for the fact her shirt had been cut and torn in half or explain the cuts on her body. This one was going to take a little more effort on his part.

Kneeling beside her, he held a large hand over her throat. An amber glow emanated from his palm and within seconds, the slice from the switchblade healed and the blood disappeared. He passed his hand over her until all the cuts healed and were clean. Staring at her shirt, he snapped his fingers. He watched the fibers weave in and out, pulling back together and mending themselves. The blood, dirt, and grime lifted and disappeared, too. Cocking his head to the side, his obsidian eyes scrutinized his handiwork. Satisfied she would find nothing about her appearance to remind her of the evening's episode, he placed his palm over her forehead. Focusing, he erased her memories of the evening, and replaced them with harmless ones of her walking home from work, sitting on the chaise for a few minutes, and innocently falling asleep. She would wake shortly, oblivious to the peril of the earlier evening.

Taking to the air, Sully flew low, heading back downtown. Walking the streets once more, he patrolled until dawn. Either the demons were lying low, or they had decided to avoid his turf. Not finding any more activity, he decided it was time to head back to his dimension. Withdrawing a small coin from his pocket, he tossed it in front of him where a portal opened, and he walked through. Enough for one night.

ABOUT THE AUTHOR

Madison Granger is a free-spirited late bloomer. She stubbornly lives by three beliefs: dreams can come true, never give up, and you're never too old to try new things. She is living proof of all three adages, vowing she isn't done by a long shot.

As a girl, she entertained her friends with stories of knights in shining armor coming to rescue the fair princess with a happy ever after. Or maybe it was their favorite rock stars falling madly in love with their giggling pre-teen selves. Either way, the stories kept them coming back for more. Today, Madison has changed brave knights and rock stars to shapeshifters and werewolves, but the happy ever after remains.

Her love of books never wavered through her life. Not ever finding the one book that told it just right, Madison decided to write it herself. The Kindred series is her "heart story" and still going strong. In between the ongoing saga of the Kindred, Madison manages to calm her muse by writing other stories. She's now added Urban Fantasy to her repertoire of Paranormal Romance.

Madison lives in southern Louisiana and enjoys reading, cheering on the New Orleans Saints, and spending time with friends and family.

Website
https://www.MadisonGranger.com/
Facebook
https://www.facebook.com/MadisonGrangerAuthor/
Twitter
https://twitter.com/MadisonGranger
Amazon
https://www.amazon.com/author/madisongranger
Goodreads
https://www.goodreads.com/author/show/15139766.Madison_Granger
Bookbub
https://www.bookbub.com/authors/madison-granger

Made in the USA
Columbia, SC
16 August 2024